Lady, Behave

Naughty Ladies
Book 2

By
Cerise DeLand

ARE YOU SIGNED UP FOR DRAGONBLADE'S BLOG?

You'll get the latest news and information on exclusive giveaways, exclusive excerpts, coming releases, sales, free books, cover reveals and more.

Check out our complete list of authors, too!

No spam, no junk. That's a promise!

Sign Up Here

www.dragonbladepublishing.com

Dearest Reader;

Thank you for your support of a small press. At Dragonblade Publishing, we strive to bring you the highest quality Historical Romance from some of the best authors in the business. Without your support, there is no 'us', so we sincerely hope you adore these stories and find some new favorite authors along the way.

Happy Reading!

CEO, Dragonblade Publishing

Additional Dragonblade books by Author Cerise Deland

Naughty Ladies Series
Lady, Be Wanton (Book 1)
Lady, Behave (Book 2)
Lady, No More (Book 3)

Chapter One

August 1815
Brighton, England

ADELAIDE DEVEREAUX PROPPED open her umbrella, stepped from the carriage, and scurried through the deluge toward the tiny chemist's shop she favored in the Lanes. Yesterday upon her perusal of the other chemist shops in this maze of little establishments, she'd discovered this charming proprietor who knew his trade better than that hum-drum chap around the corner. Cousin Cass affirmed Addy's conclusion this morning when that lovely lady who was her and her two sisters' chaperone rose from her reclining couch and declared how Mister Alworth's Fine Headache Syrup was really the best she'd ever used.

Addy knew why that was so. The addition of her own special ingredients was the reason. Mister Alworth's description of his own concoction mirrored her own requirements for excellence, save for her two little improvements. Small they might be, but it had taken her two years to perfect it. She prided herself on the success of her headache formula, as well as the other two she'd concocted in Dublin. Those two were to cure cough and loose stools. The latter was not a condition many spoke of, but one that must be corrected if one were to live serenely in polite society, eh? She often fantasized that she might one day make them remedies she could sell to the world. Of course, that would have to be after she married a man who might allow her to be so free with her knowledge and her time.

She sighed. Where would she find such a creature?

"Hurry, Fifi!" Addy dashed under the apothecary's awning as she urged Cass's French maid out of the rain.

"*Oui, Mademoiselle!!* I come!" Fifi was a cool bit of frosting, whom Cass had brought down from London two days ago when the triplets moved to Brighton to begin their debuts. The servant was forty, if a day, and took pains, or so Addy thought, to act surly. Or was the woman simply arrogantly French?

Addy pushed open the shop door and paused as Fifi scurried up behind her. The bell above the lintel ting-a-linged as both women fought to close their umbrellas, and the summer rain deluged the entry of the shop floor.

"*Quelle damage,*" Fifi complained, brushing fat raindrops from her gray pelisse and skirts.

"This is nothing, Fifi. In Ireland, it rains sheep and piglets. Here, just cats and dogs!" She chuckled at her own humor.

In reply, Fifi gave her a Gallic *hunf.*

Another good one lost on the maid. She suffered interminably from too much anxiety. Of course, Addy admitted she would, too, if she had escaped *Madame Guillotine* when she was twenty, Napoleon's Chief of Police when she was twenty-two, and a lover who had attempted to lock her in his dungeon when she was twenty-four.

"Good morning, Miss! Miss..." The shopkeeper put a finger to his temple in thought. "Adelaide Devereaux! That's it, isn't it?"

"Right you are, sir! A very good morning to you, too." Addy had no problems with men remembering her name, when they'd met or how.

"Did your cousin fare well with our headache syrup? Ah, let me recall... Don't tell me! Lady Downs, is that correct?"

Addy smiled at the man who'd been so good as to call his preparation "our" remedy. He really was a light-hearted fellow, short, portly, bald with a cute rimless pince-nez perched atop a bulbous nose. "Indeed, you have the right of it, Mister Alworth. Our guardian and cousin, Lady Downs, found the potion to be her saving grace. With the addition I recommended, of course."

"A wonderful suggestion. For one so young, you know your elixirs."

I've got the best solutions for neuritis, lung ailments, and especially for megrims, real or imagined. She shivered, satisfied with herself. "My cousin has completely recovered this morning and sends me to you with an order for another vial and her many thanks."

"Most kind of Lady Downs. Most kind." He rubbed his chubby palms together as he beamed at her. "But I am grateful to you, Miss, because it was you who had me add a drop of peppermint to my mix."

"And two of licorice, sir. Do not forget."

He leaned over his counter to focus more fully on her eyes.

Addy was used to such scrutiny of her person and did not blush but smiled graciously like the unique young creature God had seen fit to make her.

"Of course, Miss. How could I? I have often questioned if my compound was complete. One must constantly test, is that not true? So many are afflicted by these so-called lightning headaches. So hard, so very hard to cure, you know."

"I do, sir. My grandfather suffered from them, too." *Though his episodes occurred most often after a night indulging in too much good Irish whiskey.* "I had to experiment for many years to get the formula correct."

The door crashed open, and the bell rang as if it hung on a crazed cow. A roar—a wild long cry of an injured animal, tore the air and had Addy spinning toward...

The most luscious vision of a man she'd ever seen.

He was tall with a square jaw, broad brow, and a bright shock of auburn hair falling over his eyes. Handsome as any hero of Greek tragedy, he was also in distress.

One arm windmilled as he held the handle of the shop door as if it were his last sane grip on the world gone rocking.

Meanwhile his long muscular legs danced under him as he fought for purchase.

"Sir!" Addy dropped her reticule and umbrella and ran to grab his arm. She hoisted him up. Righted him. And noted by the power of his arm, he was delightfully sturdy. "Lean on me!"

He fought for words, teetering on his feet and devouring her features as if she were an angel.

Well, that was nothing new. Men did that when viewing her dulcet blue eyes and white-gold hair for the first time. She appreciated this man's good taste to marvel at her. In return, she smiled in comfort.

Clutching her arm like a pot of gold, he got his footing on the slippery floorboards. "Dear God. I say, who in hell...ah...Hades! Pardon! Pardon!"

He cleared his throat. Blinking, he recovered enough of his sanity to realize that her perfect oval face was not the one he should be addressing for redress of his grievance of the wet wooden floor. At once, he searched for the shopkeeper.

"My lord," Mister Alworth appealed to the man as he scuttled round the end of his counter. "My sincerest apologies, dear man. It is the very devil out there this morning."

"It is," the beautiful man murmured as he focused on Addy once more. "I say, good of you to help me."

"Think nothing of it, my lord. What anyone does when one slips inside a shop."

He snorted at her turn of phrase.

Good for him. She liked to surprise men with her wit. Handsome men. Like this one who was out so early in the morning. Odd for a nob to even be up at this hour and superbly dressed in expensive dark brown superfine, too. But she'd learn why and how he was out and about—and in particular, she'd discover who he was. He was too handsome, too well dressed to pass up the opportunity to give him reason to remember her.

He regained his full impressive stature and cleared his throat. But she held on to his biceps. Why not. She liked the girth. No puny boy, this man!

"I am in your debt, Miss, for your kind assistance." His gravel voice was indeed that of a hearty fellow. As he gazed down at her with his sweet chocolate eyes, she liked how he examined her in detail. "I fear we have not formally met."

"No. Perhaps Mister Alworth would do the honors for us?" She was never one to stand on too much ceremony back home in Waterford, nor even in Dublin. But here, in England, she would definitely insist on every rule to give no tongues an opportunity to wag. She was a Devereaux, one of the newly arrived grand-daughters of the late Earl of Barry, here to snare...*or ahem, no*...to find a proper husband. Rich, handsome, a man she could revere.

This excellent candidate for that honor shifted and, with an apologetic smile, bent to retrieve his top hat from the floor.

"I'm afraid that's ruined," she said with a tight press of her lips. "That is my fault."

"Never! It's only a hat."

She appreciated his ability to forgive. An excellent quality in a man.

"I say, Mister Alworth," he grinned at her, "will you help us with the proper introductions?"

"Indeed. Indeed." The little man gave a laugh, atwitter at the prospect. "I make known to you, Miss Adelaide Devereaux, this gentleman, Lord Heath."

"The Marquess of Heath, Alworth," the man corrected him with a fond smile and a bow to her. "Gyles Whitmore."

She responded with her most exquisite expression of pleasure. Wracking her brain for what she should have studied in Debrett's for the past two months, she cursed her poor memory. Had she been half as devoted as her sisters Laurel and Imogen, she'd know at once his lineage, his worth, or at least, his sire's full title. "How do you do, sir?"

"And this is Miss Adelaide Devereaux, my lord, recently come to town."

"Miss Adelaide," she corrected Alworth, allowing the more

familiar form for so marvelous a new friend as an heir to a duke. "Miss Adelaide Devereaux of the family of the Earl of Barry, of Waterford and Dublin. Lately of London and now Brighton."

She beamed as she completed the fullness of it. Heath would want to know precisely who she was and her worth. Not her financial worth. No, for that was not worth much at all. Sadly. Only two thousand. But she was the descendant of a long line of notable Norman lords who'd sailed to take Ireland after the Conqueror had claimed England.

"I am honored to make your acquaintance, Miss Devereaux. Are you in Brighton for a lengthy holiday?"

"The Season here only. Then we return to London. My two sisters and I are with our cousin, Lady William Downs."

"Ah, I know her well," her paragon said with a firm nod. "A light of London society."

Addy had perceived that when she and her sisters had lived in that city with Cousin Cass for the past few months. But it was good to hear it confirmed by another.

The door burst open with a gush of cold air and a downpour of rain. Heath hovered over her, one sturdy arm to her shoulders, as another swept into the shop with a ting-a-ling-ling-ling of the bell.

"Heath!" cried the older lady who stood in the doorway.

"Come inside, Mama!" He ceased his very welcome shelter of Addy to pull the woman into the shop and shut the door behind her with a decided thud.

"Thank you, my dear." She inched near Heath as her maid pushed into the shop and all six of them now stood indiscreetly nearly nose-to-nose. "Is this the man who sold you that syrup for our headaches?"

Addy hid her surprise. Not only was this dashing gentleman afflicted with terrible headaches as well as his mother, but the lady had admitted it aloud. Few ever wished the world to know of their maladies, especially those so high in the instep.

"Indeed, Mama."

"Good. Well!" she said with indignant authority and pushed her way past Addy to look down her nose at Mister Alworth. "I tell you, sir, your syrup does not work. It needs a stronger element. Stronger, I say!"

"Well, Your Grace, I think I have just the thing for you." He sent a thankful smile toward Addy. "If you will allow me to serve this young lady who was here before you and your son, I'll—"

"Sir!" She frowned at him and, in so doing, narrowed her long elegant nose, so similar to that of her handsome son's. "I am not accustomed to taking second place."

"No, ma'am. I understand, but—"

"I insist on good service, sir."

"And you shall have it, ma'am. But you must first understand that the excellent remedy I will give you will be superb because this young woman has improved my usual fine mixture."

"Oh?" The duchess directed her attention toward a smiling Addy. The woman's incredulous gaze spoke of a tinge of respect, just in case, Addy concluded, the lady had to praise her. "How is that possible that you should know such things?"

Addy curtsied. "My grandfather suffered such megrims, Your Grace. I was responsible for his care, and I learned the best way to treat lightning headaches by trial and error."

"Humf. And why are you here then if you know such things?" She waved a careless hand in the air denoting the shop.

"My cousin, Lady William Downs, has need of similar medication, and although I know what to put in such a potion, I am no chemist to mix it. Suffice it to say that I hope you will be discreet," Addy said with the most gratifying of dispositions cloaking the most severe warning, "and not to say that I have been so bold as to reveal her need for such to you."

"No, no. Of course not. I know of the lady, I do." The duchess pulled her pelisse closer about her chest, emphasizing that such revelation would be beneath her dignity. "Well, I should like some of your formula. I am quite ready to find relief."

Addy leaned toward the kindly apothecary. "I can certainly

wait, sir, while you fill Her Grace's order."

The little man checked the duchess's growing smile and hurried away.

Fifi's gray eyes met Addy's in praise of her largesse to allow the duchess to get her syrup first.

So did the melting brown gaze of the Marquess of Heath.

"Kind of you, young lady," announced the duchess. "Forgive me, but the shopkeeper should have introduced us."

"Indeed," said Heath. "Allow me, Mama." He proceeded to do the formalities with all names and titles included, including that of his mother, the Duchess of Stonegage.

"Devereaux." The duchess mulled over Addy's family name. "The Barrys. Quite a large family."

Addy said nothing. Well aware that a few of their distant relatives were confidants of Prince George, and scoundrels at that, she did not wish to focus on that branch of the tree. "We have many cousins in Ireland."

"And you are the branch from Waterford?"

Addy hoped that was sufficient identification. "We are."

"And your grandfather was the Earl of Barry?"

"He was."

The duchess narrowed her gaze upon Addy in a most chilling manner. "He recently passed away."

"He did. Fourteen months ago, it was." She hoped that concluded the family examination. Her grandpapa had been a loving substitute parent to the triplets after their father and mother had passed way, but outside the family, he had a less sterling reputation.

The duchess glared at her, then expressed her dim view of Grandpapa when she was so unladylike as to snort. Loudly.

Addy lost her smile. Her hope for a pleasant ending died.

The duchess went on. "Your grandfather was '*Monsieur de la Voleur de Grand Chemin.*'"

Addy noticed that the duchess had not asked a question but simply made a declaration. To cover any misinterpretation, Addy offered her own translation of Grandpapa's famous moniker. "The valet of the great road."

From the corner of the room, Fifi broke into a coughing fit.

Addy shot her a quelling look. The French woman always hated Addy's translations of her language, especially her grandfather's funny little title.

"A valet, you say?" the duchess tittered.

"*Oui*, Grandpapa was a very fine fellow. We miss him terribly."

"I'm sure you do," pronounced the woman with a tight twist of her lips. "I'm sure you do."

Silence descended over them all.

Addy tapped her toe and focused on the door to the back room.

Heath stared at Addy.

His mother gazed about the shop.

The duchess's maid and Fifi glared at each other.

Tense minutes later, Mister Alworth emerged from his back room with two vials in hand. The first, he sold to the Duchess of Stonegage, who immediately thanked him and bid all in the shop good day.

As the woman turned to leave, her son offered his thanks to Alworth. To Addy, he offered an apologetic smile and a polite bow. "A pleasure to meet you, Miss Adelaide. I hope we meet again very soon."

"As do I, my lord." She dipped in a small curtsy and prayed she'd see him soon, somewhere. When that occurred, she prayed he'd not be in the presence of his disapproving mother.

Chapter Two

HEATH SWIRLED HIS whisky and considered the choice he was about to make. The little blonde who stood across the ballroom was definitely to his taste. Smart and feminine. He liked a woman who added verve and style to the mix. Yesterday morning in that shop in the Lanes, Miss Adelaide Devereaux had proven she had pluck. She'd stood upright even after his mother took a bristle to her with her inimitable, stuffy ways. If he pursued their acquaintance, he'd send notice to Society he hunted for a wife to change his nickname from 'Blood' to 'Shackled.'

He took a swig of his drink and turned to his friend. "Join me in dancing with the ladies, will you, Martindale?"

The fellow with whom Heath had spent nearly three years in the French prison of Verdun managed a smile. "Dancing? Who has time?"

"I say, old fellow, you must give over examining the men at this party and take a good look at the finer opportunities!"

Felix Rowlandson, who had newly assumed his father's title of earl, was focused on revenging his imprisonment. The man made yet another excuse to avoid fun. His usual one was that he was seeking the person who had sent him and his father to the notice of the French gendarme in eighteen o-three.

Heath wished to lighten the mood of his friend, who had been at his particular quest for more than a decade. "Without a bit of fun, you'll lose your edge, old man."

Martindale took a long survey of the room filled with lovely young women. "Your version of fun takes too much time and, if pursued properly, would take too much of my money to truly make me happy."

"Oh, I dunno. I'd gladly spend my wealth on a fine bit of muslin if she devoted her wits to my welfare." *Miss Adelaide, for example. A Diamond by her looks. A canny bit by her actions.* "Would you possibly interest yourself in three ladies who appear to be the mirror image of each other?"

Heath narrowed his gaze on a set of three young women standing with an older one in the far corner. Adelaide stood with them, two of whom were so near her good looks that they had to be sisters. One had golden tresses. One, red-gold. And the other woman with them was their chaperone, the good-looking society maven, Lady William Downs.

"One of them," Martindale admitted, "is quite fetching."

"Which?" asked Heath, hoping his friend favored one of the others and not his charming Adelaide.

"The one in peach."

"I prefer the one in pink."

"She's the spitting image of their mother," Lex offered.

"Glorious blonde hair," Heath murmured. "But that lady is not their mother."

"No? A duenna?"

"Hardly. That's Lady Downs. Lady William Downs." Heath grinned. "A leading light in London society. And a widow."

"Is that so?" Felix brightened, discerning a note of Heath's sexual interest. "Know her well, do you?"

"Well enough." He laughed. "No, Lex. I don't favor her. I like her, yes. But she's many years my senior."

"When was age ever a deterrent?"

"Stop." Heath put aside his glass on a nearby footman's tray. "You think me more jaded than I am."

Heath liked women. When Lex and he had lived in Paris while Bony was in Elba, Heath had availed himself of two French mistresses. His wealth from his estates and his status this past year as a diplomat had allowed him the pick of the demimonde. Happily, what he'd learned about how to seduce a woman could fill books. Getting a wife, which was why he'd allowed himself to be persuaded to come to Brighton this month, was not his usual pastime. But his parents demanded he pay regard to it. He was, as his father pointed out, aged thirty-three. His health, never the best since his abuse by the French, demanded he think of getting an heir. And soon.

He wished he could encourage his oldest friend to find a bit of fun in life, too. Words, however, tended to fall deaf on Lex's ears. After a few more tries, Heath suggested Lex needed to smile. Think of women and babies.

He promised he would. "I'm close to learning who sold my father and me."

Heath cursed. "I hope to God that's true. I'm tired of watching you track each suspect. It's eating up your youth."

"No one sold *you* into prison, my friend."

"I was condemned just the same," Heath said between clenched teeth. *The anxiety gave me ripping headaches that can send me to my knees.* "I could hope to find each of Napoleon's guards who pointed his rifle at my guts and poked me along the roads east. But what good will it do me, eh? I am done with it. I want to live the life I was born to. I want you to live yours, too."

"I have only one suspect left. I'm closing in on him. As soon as I obtain proof, I shall confront him. Then I'm done with revenge. I'm on to women. A wife. An heir. Just like you!"

Heath wished to obliterate the memories of the squalor and starvation they'd endured in captivity. "I give you until Christmas. Then I want to see a new man."

"You will." Lex put his hand on Heath's shoulder. "Go now. Pick one of those three lovelies."

His friend checked his expression. Then he shifted to better avail himself of a glimpse of the three. He wanted to claim Adelaide for himself, but Lex had hardly ever allowed himself the joy of pursuing a woman who'd be a proper fit. "I don't know which one to choose first."

"Oh, yes, you do." Lex insisted. "Ask her to dance. Make your father and mother happy."

"I mustn't look too interested." Heath swung his gaze toward his parents, who stood talking with the host and hostess of this evening's ball. He'd gotten an earful of scurrilous nonsense from his mother yesterday after their shop visit about the notorious Barry family. Her warnings about the "nefarious" grandfather, who was deceased, sounded like a whine.

His father had put her up to it, as ever when the duke wanted Gyles to do his bidding. Usually, he did not find too much fault with that, but this request cut deeper. This Barry girl had a carefree charm that made him smile. "I love them dearly, but they've become fanatics about my need to marry. One dance, and my mother wants to check the poor girl's teeth. Papa would ask for her sire and dam."

With a grin, Lex extended a hand toward the floor.

Heath would indeed pursue his quest of lovely Adelaide. "Well, since you won't indulge yourself, I shall have to uphold all British manhood." Heath clapped him on the shoulder. "Wish me luck."

ADELAIDE TOOK THE introduction of Cousin Cass to the scrumptious Marquess of Heath with the cool demeanor of one who knew her looks could enchant. She'd caught men's attention before without trying. She'd rather not have to try too much with him, for there was an essence of him that spoke of his natural affinity for her. As if they fit together like two pieces of a puzzle.

The other truth was that he was appealingly masculine, virile, yet vulnerable. Handsome and debonair, titled, too, yet he held a silent storm within him. Headaches such as he endured came to one who had suffered physically or even mentally over a period of time. That human frailty she found intriguing in a man so otherwise confident. It was a quality that endeared him to her, imperfect as she also was.

"I'm very pleased to find you here." He took her hand and led her away from her family toward the dance floor.

"And I, you, my lord." She liked a man with honesty in his soul. With the awareness that many young ladies in the ballroom noted them, she relished his invitation.

Not only had he remembered her from the shop, but his request improved her reputation. Interesting that he had maintained the illusion with Cass that Addy had just now been introduced to him. He'd not let on to Cass that they had a prior meeting, and she had not brought up the matter. Cass would have asked questions, and Addy supposed that the reason Heath did not wish to have their previous introduction known was the existence of his headaches.

The orchestra began, and he bowed before her as the other male dancers did to their partners. "I'm glad of it."

Her heart pounded. She was proud to hear him compliment her so.

"I must thank you for your addition to Alworth's syrup."

"It worked well for your mother?"

"Indeed." The dancers in their set began a rhythmic walk to the right. Heath's commanding arm around her waist felt comforting against the silk of her gown. "It worked in minutes. I thought it...magic."

He had tried it, too? Wonderful! "You approve!"

"I do. Have you perhaps training in chemistry, Miss Adelaide?"

She admired the melting regard of his gaze. It was rather like jumping into a cup of hot chocolate. She'd like to kiss his eyelids. Taste his long dark auburn lashes. Lick the cinnamon spicing the brew.

He grinned at her as they turned, and she caught the sensuous lure of his perusal. "Do you?"

"Do I...? I'm sorry. I had a moment's distraction."

"So did I, Miss Adelaide." He said with that bass voice that tingled her toes. "I look at you and see all's right with the world."

Now she'd heard men go into raptures about her before. Her hair was an angel's. Her eyes, the morning sky. Her skin, the...whatever it was. Parchment. Vanilla. Something, something. But this from him in his stirring bass voice sounded so sincere, she could not count it down as hard seduction.

"I find you intriguing," she'd said as they returned to each other, and she met his forthright gaze with her own. "Forgive me. I say what I know. Am I too bold?"

His manly features mellowed. So he was in earnest. Not simply the swain, the seducer, the rogue who would sweet-talk her. "Please. Continue."

"You have schooled yourself to a serene exterior. You control your days, your nights, your friends. Yet you have suffered greatly."

He stared at her so fiercely, she could not tell if he was shocked or complimented by her insights. "You heard my mother declare it."

"More than headaches, I venture." She tipped her head as she regarded him with compassion. Her truths could send others fleeing her, never to return. Revealing herself to this man would test his mettle. Her hope to keep him interested could die on this dance floor. "I have a skill to see the pain people bear beneath their visage."

They left each other at the march of the dance, and when they came round again, he gripped one of her hands as dictated by the form, but his hold was that of a desperate man's. "How do you come by it? Your grandfather taught you? Your mother? Who?"

"None. Perhaps it was my attachment to Grandpapa's maladies that opened my sensitivities to others' complaints. I only know I can see beneath the surface. Your mother, for example—"

And they parted once more.

"Tell me," he murmured when they faced each other again.

"She has megrims." Addy spun away. And when she returned, she said, "But I think she has more. A palsy. St. Vitus Dance, perhaps?"

"How do you see this?" he urged, appearing awed as well as rabid to learn more of her abilities.

"Your mother's right hand shakes when she wishes to be emphatic. This is not normal. Not even though she wishes to draw attention to her desires. I'd say she needs oranges and more sunshine."

Once more they were parted by the steps of the country dance.

And when together again, he leaned close and whispered, "I wish to hear more about your abilities, Miss Adelaide."

"Addy," she told him on impulse, hoping that he might feel comfortable describing how or why he acquired his debilitating health condition. Men disliked claiming any malady, noting any as their failure.

"Gyles," he responded and grinned at her. "We will be fast friends."

"Shall we declare it already so?" To wipe away any formalities would speed their courtship if indeed she still liked him after this dance.

"We are. I wish to see you again, Addy. Quite soon."

Quivering in success, Addy knew precisely where and when. "Do come to tea. We receive on Wednesdays, Thursdays, and Fridays."

"I will be there tomorrow."

She could barely breathe. To secure the friendship of such a dashing creature on her first night out made her head spin. "You will?"

"I make no promises I do not keep, Addy."

"We should be delighted to have you. Tomorrow. Any day. Every day." She hesitated for a moment, then did as he had bid her and called him by his given name. "Gyles."

The musicians wound to the conclusion of their tune while the pair of them smiled at each other like two court jesters.

"We are in a house off the Marine Parade," she told him as they ended their dance. "At number twenty Charles Street."

From the corner of her eye, Addy detected the scrutiny of his mother. The duchess was not happy to see her son in Addy's company. But her reputation was spotless. Utterly! Not even her sisters, Laurel and Imogen, were as unblemished. Surely, Grandpapa was not so ignoble as the good lady presumed. What did it matter that he had acquired a few items that were not his own? That he had profited from their keeping and their sale? He was not as scurrilous as many? Why, were there not scoundrels of every noble title in this very ballroom? In this seaside town?

A high sharp shriek from an instrument rent the air.

Gyles winced and slapped his hand to his forehead. "What in hell is that?" he asked as cymbals clashed and rang as they hit the floor.

"A violinist mis-struck his bow," Addy told him and led him away from the dancers, her arm wound in his. "A tympanist lost his cymbals. They're both fine. But you are not. Come with me to the chairs."

Pale, panting for air, his eyes closed, he walked along with her. With each step, he fought to move with ease, but still, he stumbled twice.

Sitting beside him, Addy held his hand, no matter propriety. He needed her. She knew enough of his malady to sit for many minutes without a word between them. He recovered himself, but slowly. And when a footman approached with a tray of wine or whiskey on offer, Gyles would have taken one.

"Do not," she admonished.

He stared at her. "No?"

"Spirits will only aggravate your condition."

He looked away but grimaced at the bright light of candles in a nearby sconce.

"Close your eyes. Turn toward me." She stroked his hand and wrapped her fingers around his wrist and counted. "There. Your heartbeat slows. You will be well. Give this a few minutes."

He did as she bade him, and in his time, he opened his eyes to consider her with quiet appreciation shining there. "You know my condition."

"Bold sounds. Bright lights. Alcohol. Late nights. Exertion. They all contribute to your headaches. How long have you suffered them?"

He exhaled. "Since I was imprisoned by the French when I was young."

"I see." She squeezed his hand in sympathy. About that, she would learn more but not tonight. He had to recover first before he relived the cause of his distress. "You should not be at balls, sir. But home where you can be quiet and untroubled."

"But if I did not attend here tonight, I would not have found you again."

She bobbed her head to and fro. "We might have met in more sedate gatherings."

"Perhaps. I would have chanced missing you."

She had never been so sweetly entranced by a man who confessed to his liking for her in so unique a manner. "My sisters and I are in Brighton specifically to enjoy the Season. We will be…" she said as she circled a hand in the air, "everywhere."

"Addy, how may I press my advantage?"

"You made an impression on me yesterday, Gyles. I will not soon forget you."

He grasped her hand tightly. "Don't forget me at all."

"I won't. How could I? You like my syrup." She had to tease him and make him smile.

"I do. Among other things."

She nodded, compassion in her heart for so afflicted a darling man. "Perhaps my dancing, too?"

"Indeed," he said. "I'd like to kiss you for it."

She gave a shocked little laugh. Since Grandpapa died and she knew she'd have to find a husband soon, she'd taken to kissing any man who appealed. Alas, she'd found none. But now, she was not only complimented but tempted to kiss this man. "Not here."

"No. But somewhere and soon. With my thanks for the syrup, the dance, and the laughter."

Oh, my. Was he much too chivalrous? Was he a rake of no morals? A man who complimented women? Women like her? Young and naive. For all her good looks, for all her pride in them and understanding of them as a tool to attract men, she was still untried, uninformed of much of the physicality of mating. She could be all too easily influenced by a practiced man's charms. Of that, she had always been on guard.

"A kiss for relief from a headache? Oh, surely that would be—"

"Bliss," he vowed. "I will try for it tomorrow."

"When you come for tea?"

"I come for you, Addy."

He lifted her hand and pressed his firm lips to her glove in a stunning kiss. Had he blessed her bare skin with his mouth, she would have taken him to an alcove in the hall and tasted the flavor of his desire and called herself barely satisfied.

"Tomorrow then," she whispered and longed to taste his lips on hers.

Chapter Three

Royal Pavilion
Brighton

"MAMA!" HEATH FOUND his mother in his sitting room, a surprise considering she usually retired from such events before midnight. It was a wonder she'd even found his rooms in the maze that was Prinny's mash-mash, Chinese-Mughol, favorite residence. For the past five days and nights, Heath had had a devil of a time finding the path himself, let alone scaring up a footman who knew his way to the back of beyond. Now Heath was in no mood for arguing with her. But she stayed atop all the best gossip, so he could predict the matter that stuck in her craw. *As if I can avoid discussing it.* "You're not abed. Are you ill?"

She stared up at him from the wing chair next to the fire. "Where've you been?"

"Actually, my dear, I've been wandering the damn halls of this labyrinth. If I'd known that the honor of being Prince George's guest in his Pavilion would be a treasure hunt, I'd have taken a room on the Steine!"

"Oh, hush! You ungrateful boy. Rooms here are such an honor. Hard to come by, too. And your father is thrilled."

"And lucky for him, already abed. I say, Mama, why are you here? Ill? Need my supply of headache syrup?"

"I am not ill, you rascal. And well you know it."

"I know no such thing." He shrugged from his formal frock coat and folded it over the back of a chair. "Hurry on with the scolding, will you, please. I am very tired."

"You know why I'm here." She wiggled her shoulders in indignation.

"If I do, then you've no reason to be here. You can retire, and we can avoid any repetition of our previous contretemps."

"Don't be impertinent."

He ran a hand through the shock of his hair at his brow. "Shall I say it for you?"

She huffed and fixed him with her stern umber gaze. "I told you I do not approve of those Barry girls."

"Because of their grandfather. Yes. What did he do, my dear?" Heath always loved to hear the rationale behind his father's disapproval of others. This of the elder Barry sounded hollow, indefensible as it was—given it was his father—the pot calling kettle black. "Attempt to seduce you before you were married to Papa?"

"Oh!" She took umbrage, turned red, and pulled up the collar of her purple velvet dressing gown. "Never. I would not—"

"Not allow it," he said, softening his disapproval of her carrying his father's complaint to him. "I know, sweet. I know. Just tell me the full of it, will you, so that we can each climb into our respective beds and dream?"

"You'll not dream of her."

But I wish to. Shocking that, given his previous taste for the talented women of London. "Why? You must tell me more than simply warning me away."

"She is not suitable."

"An earl's granddaughter meets the standard of a marquess." He undid a few buttons of his waistcoat and brushed his hand down his thigh as he crossed one leg over the other. *Her looks sear my brain with their perfection, and her forthright manner thrills my world-weary soul.* "I like her eligibility and her aplomb."

"A duchess needs more than that to be a proper spouse."

He knit his brows. His mother would have her due or take longer to acquire it than if he simply let her have her head. But he was very tired of her pressing him on the issue. "A marchioness needs style. Gravitas. An understanding of her role in the world and in her husband's estates. I can attest to Miss Adelaide possessing the first two. We might imagine what good she could accomplish on the estate of a man who owns eleven thousand acres and has administration of eighty-eight tenants."

"Someday, the future duchess of Stonegage will have twice that to attend to."

"Not soon, Mama. The current duchess is hale and hearty. Feisty, too. She takes on her son in the middle of the night when he is quite exhausted and needs his bed."

She raised a hand.

"But!" He interrupted her attempt to take charge. "You will have your way. I'd like to oblige you. Unfortunately, I've talked with her and learned much of her, more than you know. You cannot talk me out of this!"

"She's lovely. I grant you. But in her veins flows the blood of a villain."

He winced. "A bit strong, wouldn't you say, for one so young and beautiful?"

"You know the Barrymores are friends with the Regent."

"Distant cousins, are they not?"

She nodded, her nostrils pinched at the mention of three brothers who had caroused with Prinny and even pimped, it was said, for him.

"And the Earl of Barry who left his mortal coil a year ago was estranged from those infamous others, as I understand it. So what did he do, Mama? Eh? Fight with Papa? Over what? Or buy horses out from under you? Might he have done worse and sold my whereabouts to the French twelve years ago? You know that my friend the Earl of Martindale and his father were betrayed to the local *gendarme*."

"No. Not any of that. Your capture was accidental. Serendipity. Not like that poor man and his son, your friend."

"Well, out with the reason! Because unless you can tell me the old earl murdered someone and his dead son, too, we will not speak of this again."

"The son was blameless."

"I see," Heath said, his patience thinning. "Good to know. So the grandfather was...?"

"A crook."

"All right!" He inhaled. So many men were crooks these days. Taking what did not belong to them. Women, money, advantages. "And he was a gambler? A horse thief? A what?"

"A fence."

Heath stared at her. His mother was a striking, lovely woman. With red-gold hair, even at her age of fifty-five, she had skin that glowed clear and pink. She smiled, and the world smiled with her. She frowned, and she took your skin off. Do her wrong, and she never forgot or forgave. There was much more here than her simple declarations of the old earl's criminal behavior. What was it? "Very well, Mama. The old man was a fence. Of what?"

"Paintings, sculpture, jewelry. Oh, not the small trifles. Not rings or stick pins."

"But of watercolors and portraits? Parures? Rubies from India?"

"Yes! Diamonds and sapphires worth fortunes," she confirmed.

"Yours?" he asked because this was where this was going, wasn't it?

"No."

Heath waited. No words were forthcoming. "I take it then that you want something the old earl possessed."

"Your father does."

"What?"

"A portrait of his great-great-grandmother. The first Countess of Stonegage."

Of this young woman, Heath had heard. She'd been a beauty, a blonde with large blue eyes and a fulsome figure, the daughter of a landed baron who attracted the attentions of none other than the randy King of England, Henry Tudor, the eighth ruler of that name. She had returned the affections of the king, married though she was. It was even passed down as gospel, father to son in the family, that she was the first to establish the Whitmore trait of licentiousness.

His mother gazed into the dark fireplace, trying as she always did to hide her distaste for her husband's family follies. "The portrait used to hang in Stonegage Priory until thirty-five years ago."

A year after his parents' marriage then. Heath had a few ideas how the painting had trotted off to Ireland. All of them involved money, or rather, its lack. "At which time, it migrated to the Dublin house of the Earl of Barry. Why?"

"Your father was required to pay a debt."

"A large one."

She nodded. "Barry paid the fine and fee."

"Is this portrait worth a lot of money now?"

"Indeed, it is." She lifted her gaze to his.

"The painter? Who was it, Mama?"

"Holbein."

Suddenly his father was a connoisseur of Renaissance art? He stifled the urge to laugh.

There was more to this than family pride or covetousness. Whatever the cause, that was his father's problem.

Heath could not give a fig.

No. 20 Charles Street
Brighton

AFLOAT WITH THE attentions of the Marquess of Heath on her first evening into society, Addy sailed up the stairs to the dressing room she shared with her two sisters. Imogen and Laurel ran behind her. Cousin Cass had remained at the ball deeper into the night and urged the young women to return home earlier than she to recuperate for their first "at home" tomorrow.

"We were a triumph!" Addy rejoiced as she swept open the door for Laurel and Imogen.

"You were," Laurel declared with a sigh of resignation. "And Imogen, too."

"You could be, too," Addy replied. Laurel had not been her cheery self since a gentleman she adored had turned his favor toward a young woman his parents demanded he wed. Soon after, their grandfather had died, and the three girls had sunken into grief for the kindly fellow. "A smile costs so little and brings such rewards."

Imogen shook her head at Addy. She had failed lately to urge Laurel from her brown study, so Imogen had given up.

Addy was nothing if not persistent. "Remember, Laurel. We are here. We are lovely. Rich. And we are virgins. Or as close to it as possible." She cast a teasing glance at Imogen.

"We are!" Imogen shot both palms in the air, alarmed. "We are! I am! I keep telling you!"

"I believe you, dearest," Addy replied and patted her hand.

Imogen huffed. "I tell you, I am whole! Intact! But I must get out of this darned corset!"

Fifi rushed forward to undo Imogen's gown.

She stood still as the maid worked her laces. "Argh! Listen to me, both of you. I am whole. Really! That fellow Wye who accosted me in that garden in Dublin did *not* ruin me! Not then. Not tonight either. He was there. Did you see him?"

Addy said, "I did, and I worried."

"No need to. I cut him. Straight away. The cur!"

"We know, dear." Laurel threw a consoling look at Imogen but knit her brows. "As to rich, Addy? Really, you must not say that. We are frau—"

"Stop that!" Addy said, furious that Laurel kept calling the three of them frauds.

What if Grandpapa had once run a profitable fencing ken? He hadn't diddled poor folks out of a shilling or drawn the King's picture in bad ink to twiddle the currency. For many years he'd made a profit, dealing in prime goods, selling a good product for a decent price. He never nipped or shaved a crimp just to have one over on him. She knew because she'd heard him make deals with his cons. And he always asked for the provenance of paintings and statues. Old gold coins, too.

Grandpapa accepted nothing less than real goods, sort of...or nearly honestly come by. What's more, she'd seen his collection. Beauties, they were. She'd never told her sisters that she'd viewed the piles and stacks of goods in his secret storeroom in the Dublin manse. Nor would she let on. Sleeping dogs, she believed, should snore on.

Shooing away Laurel's accusations, she bent over to pucker her lips at the mirror. Tonight, she hadn't tried them out on any man. A shame. A girl needed experience kissing. Except, of course, she should be saving herself for the luscious marquess, Gyles, who promised to kiss her soon...if she didn't kiss him first. "Indeed, my dears," she told her sisters, "we are the cream of the Irish."

Laurel wrinkled her nose.

"I saw that," Addy proclaimed, then proceeded to pluck the pins from her platinum tresses. "What I don't understand is how Grandpapa's coffers, which were so full when we were young, were at his death, so empty. Except for our dowries, or course."

Imogen drew back with this odd look on her face. "I agree. His sudden poverty doesn't make any sense. We all know that Grandpapa was a famous—"

Laurel shot a wide-eyed glare at Imogen.

And Addy caught the warning look.

"Man." Imogen coughed. "A famous man! He was. Sorry. Ahem. Ugh. Something stuck in my throat."

Like the word "thief"? Their eighty-year-old grandfather was reputed to be the greatest fencer in Ireland. But her sisters thought Addy innocent of the family tendency to...*ahem*...acquire items that did not belong to them. She did have some ability at the French language, but she feigned much of it when it came to the moniker and the respectability of Grandpapa. Now that their future depended on spotless reputations, she'd keep up the illusion of propriety. "We all know that the famous last Earl of Barry was a kind and generous man."

"*Ah, Monsieur le Comte de Barrie etait célèbre.*" Fifi mumbled to herself in that raspy voice that she must've stolen from the bottom of a French brandy barrel. "*Monsieur de la Voleur de Grand Chemin.*"

Imogen frowned at the French woman.

To which, Fifi shrugged like an indifferent cat.

"*Oui, Fifi.*" Addy, joyous at the servant's interruption, gave diversion from the horrid truth. "Famous. 'The valet of the great road.' No matter his money problems at the end. We must remember the splendid upbringing he gave us. And applaud him for the dowries for our future."

Laurel and Imogen exchanged looks that might have frozen the English Channel.

However, Addy dismissed their inability to see the bright side of this. She preferred to focus on the present and the future. And the Marquess of Heath.

Addy had work to do to discover a way to keep that marvelous fellow enthralled. Aside from talking of headache remedies and kissing him, which was always dangerous. She wanted to know more about his deprivations and the conditions that had led to his malady. She intended to show him her other serious attributes, and he might remain interested in her.

Oh, bugger, that men could be fickle. Especially with young women who were good-looking and assumed to have cotton for brains.

Chapter Four

"**I**'M GLAD YOU'VE come with me today," Gyles told his friend Lex, the Earl of Martindale. They'd left the Pavilion in Gyles's coach and headed for Charles Street in a pounding rainstorm. "I do believe you have been missed these past two days at tea."

"I had business to attend to," Lex told him with a sigh of satisfaction. "I may have new evidence that will lead me to the scoundrel who sold my father and me to the French."

"That's what you were doing in Shoreham the other day?"

"I was."

"Better to sprinkle pleasure in with that tedious search for a culprit," Gyles said with hope to lure his friend from his quest.

"I agree. I need to take my mind from this, or it will eat me alive. And I do wish to see Miss Imogen again. Speaking of which," Lex added with a grin. "You say this is the third day you've gone to tea at Lady Downs's home? Are your intentions toward one special lady not too apparent?"

"They are." With that stunning platinum hair and those exquisite blue eyes, he had discovered he wanted her wit as well, not just in his bed but at his breakfast table, too. "I enjoy Adelaide's conversation."

"Enough to give the charming little blonde the assumption that an offer is forth-coming?"

Gyles nodded, a familiar stirring in his loins at the prospect of her in his arms once more. "If I continue to be amused, an offer may well come."

Lex blurted out an astonished laugh. "I'm shocked. You! A confirmed rake! Do you not have two ladies established in London?"

"I haven't seen them in months."

"They bore you?"

"I find I need...something more these days. Serenity, quiet companionship." Addy's prescription fit his mood. She'd also fit so well against his loins. Lithe, sinuous, and willing. "The very reason I visit Prinny's little abode is because my parents want me to do the Season here. They want babies, preferably male, very soon." *Even if they do not wish the bride to be the lovely Miss Adelaide Devereaux.*

The next morning after Gyles's argument with his mother, he had told his father to have the Holbein returned to him in the usual manner. "Buy it."

"But how, boy? God's teeth, Barry is dead. Who knows what has happened to the portrait now?"

"Simple. Ask his solicitor, Father."

"But...but...who in hell knows who that is?" the duke ranted on.

"Oh, for heaven's sake. Ask your man to inquire in the city. Someone knows. Spread the word and say you want to buy it!"

"I will not." Stonegage stuck out his formidable jaw.

"Why not?"

"It was stolen from me."

"Mama suspects you sold it for debts."

The duke waved that explanation away. "No matter! I will not lower myself to buy it back."

"The Earl of Barry lies six feet under. He will never know you paid for it."

"I refuse to do it."

"Then, Father, do without."

"I cannot! It's the fulfillment of a lifetime to have it back. My pride's at stake! I tell you, I will make those girls' lives a misery if I cannot have it for my own."

Gyles had burned with fury at the threat. "Do not even think it, Father. I will fight you tooth and nail if you hurt the Devereauxs."

The duke, in his youth a happy rake, was becoming a vengeful and surly roué.

Gyles directed his attention to Lex, who settled more deeply into the squabs and rambled on about the values of wedded bliss versus their own bachelorhood. "You're only thirty-three, Gyles. I thought you were waiting to marry in your dotage. Continue to be the Blood of London!"

"Ha. Ha." He flexed his fingers, considering his gold and ruby signet ring—and how he could make finer use of it as a wedding ring to take Addy to his heart and his bed. "She makes me laugh."

Lex glanced out the window at the rain, his expression changing from gloom to joy. "A good thing. I found it true myself the other night with her sister, Imogen. Perhaps humor is a family trait."

"Inherited, too, do you suppose?" Gyles liked that idea. "I could do with that."

"It's no small talent to bring a smile to someone's face. Especially yours and mine," Lex said with the dismal days of their imprisonment in Verdun darkening Gyles's visage.

"I've spent years reliving them. I know, I know. I escaped long before you, so what have I to complain about, eh? Whereas you endured that hell for nearly four years. Then stayed on to spy for eight more! Meanwhile, your poor father stayed and died there."

"It was as he wanted. He knew the composition of the rock, the consistency of the earth around the bed of the Meuse. He had studied in his youth the rich loam on the fringe of the Argonne forest. When we were marched there to the dungeons of the Citadel, he never feared. He encouraged each of us to be of good cheer. He told us he knew the means to gain our freedom."

"I remember him as so confident we could escape," Gyles said with a wistful sigh. "I arrived in Verdun more than a month later than you. Both of you were weary and cold, bony with hunger, and yet your father bade us all smile and sing each time the guards served us their tasteless gruel."

Lex's father, then in his forties, had been a strong, proud blustery fellow. Captured by the French *gendarme* in Normandy when someone betrayed their attempt to return to England after Napoleon canceled the Amiens Treaty, the then earl of Martindale and his son, sixteen-year-old Felix, were marched across the breadth of France to the frontier fortress of Verdun.

Over the next six years until his death, the earl was the one who headed the construction of the prisoners' escape tunnel. As an amateur engineer, he understood how to dig out the earth, how to hide it, funnel its course, and how to deflect it from the river that could flood it. When the tunnel collapsed, as it often did, in flood or after mudslides, he knew how to repair it or redirect the remains. He would not leave there but insisted all others go before him—even his son. When the old earl died, he had helped more than thirty British to escape the clutches of the French guards.

In June of eighteen-fourteen, as Napoleon took up exile in Elba, Gyles had met Lex in Paris, and the two of them had gone to Verdun. There, they spent more than a month searching for the grave where the guards had buried the old earl and two of their fellow prisoners. They found his remains outside the walls of a fort high in the hills above the city. There the two built a decent gravesite for the man who had saved so many, marking his earthly resting place nearest to the sky where Lex hoped his father could envision his native land.

"Your father was a hero to so many of us," Gyles told him. "May we all live with half as much nobility of character."

"He'd like it if we lived well to celebrate his sacrifice." Lex reached for his top hat and flicked off a bit of lint. "I know my father would like Imogen. Laughter is good medicine. It's even more attractive in a woman."

"No palliative needed for so engaging a character," Gyles agreed and caught up his own hat as his coach stopped before the rented house of Lady William Downs. "Complaints and demands are more the norm in the women I have all too often thought attractive. But I've decided these past few days that conversations in bed about money and jewels are extremely tiresome."

"Whatever can you mean?" Lex feigned shock. "In bed, I like to discuss my estate profits!"

"The hell you do!" Gyles slapped him on the back. "Let's go inside and laugh!"

⇒⇒⇒⇐⇐⇐

VISCOUNT HEWETT OF Hartwing Hall in Yorkshire was a pleasant fellow who had come early today and, as he had yesterday, attached himself to Addy forthwith. He was another conquest, and she needed to be able to choose the best man to wed among those attracted to her. But Gyles was the one she wanted.

At the moment, however, Hewett demanded her full attention. He was a talker, chattering on about himself. While that was tolerable, his eyes strayed to her bodice. His beady-eyed interest made her squirm. Those assets of hers, which Fifi called a woman's *choux*, were nicely shaped but were apples compared to those that Imogen sported. If Hewett had an appetite for her—or any man did—Addy hoped it was because of what she had in her head, not on her chest.

Still, she was polite to him. Why not? Cousin Cass had told her last night after they reviewed all the men who had attended tea yesterday that Hewett might have a reputation as a rogue, but he also had eight-thousand a year income from a profitable country estate. That, plus his ownership of a large old townhouse in Mayfair, made Hewett more financially viable than the third man who paid Addy special court, the congenial Duke of

32

Lonsdale.

Yet Gyles, as Marquess of Heath, was the richer. In land, he held twice as much. Income, enough to fund his own houses in London and Yorkshire, plus he often footed his father's debts. With a sterling reputation as a former prisoner of Bony's, a spy for the Crown, and a diplomat for Whitehall, Gyles was the man with the most favorable assets. That he was also called the Blood of the Season for his rakish ways saddened her. She'd not tolerate a husband who wandered or gambled or drank. Yet her first impression of him had not flagged him as a scoundrel. Could she count on her insight to confirm him as a fine man?

"What do you think, Miss Adelaide?" Hewett called her back from her wool-gathering.

"I do, indeed. Think, that is. Of course."

Arching a skeptical brow, he nonetheless continued on about his physical prowess, of all things.

She smiled, letting him rave on.

Where was Gyles?

She glanced toward the parlor door. He'd been so prompt the previous two days. She grew irritable.

Meanwhile, Imogen paced the floor in front of the parlor window.

Addy sympathized with her sister and shot to her feet. With excuses to Hewett, she left him.

Cousin Cass was urging Imogen away from her vigil at the window. "We don't want our guests to detect your anxiety."

Addy gave her sister a smile. "Imogen's fearful Martindale won't come again today."

"I thought he was committed," Imogen murmured.

Laurel sat near the window and leaned close to put in, "There are so many others who have accepted. You mustn't be dismayed, Imogen."

Imogen and Addy examined Laurel's smile. This was the first sign of a sunnier sister...and welcome, no matter the reason.

"He was forthright," Imogen added, her gaze lingering on the rain.

"Perhaps his friend, the Marquess of Heath, will attend again and share news of him," Addy said, trying to help. "I can ask."

"Never," Cousin Cass whispered harshly. "Martindale sent his regrets for both days. We shall welcome him at any time."

"Do not fret, Imogen." Addy pleaded. "He may appear at the yachting party tomorrow!"

"But I won't," Imogen said. "One foot on that boat, and I'll toss my breakfast over everyone!"

"Really, dear!" Cass shivered. "We needn't be reminded of how you cannot stand the sea!"

"Well, then he'll certainly attend the Carstairs' reception in the Steine." Addy bubbled with anticipation at the next most prominent event they'd attend a few nights hence.

"A carriage is stopping." Imogen squinted through the rain-splashed window.

Addy bent over but could not see through the raindrops on the panes. "The colors of it are—?"

"Indigo with yellow lacquer." Imogen sighed.

"Heath!" Addy hoisted her skirts and headed for the hall.

"Serenity, Adelaide," Cass warned as if she were the queen.

Sounds of their new butler opening the front door floated up the staircase. Melodious male voices exchanged pleasantries, and footsteps heralded the arrival of two guests. Addy rushed forward, Imogen behind her. Heath and Martindale left off their hats and coats and umbrellas. The sisters led the men up the stairs into the salon, where promptly, others seized their attention and took them away.

Addy surrendered to finding herself locked in a conversation with Lonsdale, Hewett, and another fellow who was a baronet from Winchester. Only when Cass interrupted and began a conversation with the duke and the viscount about Prinny's tastes in architecture, did Addy find chance of relief. She rose and made her way to an empty chair before the fire. There within a minute, Gyles bowed before her.

"I'm so happy to see you again, my lord." Addy flushed with delight that he had come to her. He was so dashing in a forest green frockcoat, copper satin waistcoat, and fawn breeches. "Do sit with me by the fire? It's chilly today."

He agreed and took the chair next to hers. "I like a good blaze. Even in summer. It is one thing I demand of every room in my homes."

She saw the dark memories of his imprisonment flash over his countenance. "To keep warm is a good choice. One can remove clothes easily."

"But often one cannot don enough layers to ward off the cold."

"A chill invades the bones and the heart. In Ireland," she said, "the winds from the sea can unnerve a body. The storms come this way and that, a gentle patter or the drum of thunder and lightning all in a minute. I'm glad you keep yourself warm. You will live long and well to have done so."

"But you lived near the sea."

"We did. It has its rewards. The crisp air. The skyline view of forever and beyond. The constant rhythm of the surf upon the shore that keeps time of the racing minutes you are allotted on this earth."

"Would you ever consider a life away from the sea?"

What was he asking her? She'd be a fool to infer too much into such a question. Yet her heart pounded at the possibility he might hint at such interest in her. "I would. Although I'd like to visit the seaside now and then. I love to watch how people absorb the sun and play in the sand. I confess that I like to bathe in it, too."

"So do I." He chuckled with her. "Some say humans came from the sea. I can believe it. We are more than blood and bone." He drifted off again into the reverie where he could sink and disappear from her.

"We are." She covered his hand with her own. "We are invited to the Rensfords' Regatta tomorrow. Do you go? Do you like to sail?"

"I do attend. I like such events very much, though I doubt I'd ever spend my time or energy buying a yacht or sailing one. I do like to sail on others' boats."

She sighed in satisfaction and allowed herself the enjoyment of conversing with him. He was such a different model of a man compared to Hewett or weak-chinned Lonsdale.

"I note how popular you are," he said, his face solemn.

"I do enjoy learning about others."

"Do you like Hewett? Or Lonsdale?"

Jealousy in man was not attractive—and never had she encouraged it. Nor would she ever speak against a guest. "Gentlemen, each. I find their company pleasing."

He held her gaze like a key in a lock. "I apologize. I go about this the wrong way."

"Go about what?"

"Telling you that I feel the sting of competition."

Ah, she saw his problem and softened. "Never had it, have you?"

He looked away and back to meet her frankly. "No, I never have. Except for the few years I was in prison in Verdun, I have had everything I ever wanted. At my fingertips, instantly."

"Well," she said and drew herself up into her dignity, "many of us have not had that privilege."

He winced. "I see I need to acquire humility."

A spark of humor lit in her veins. "A fine trait."

He shook his head, smiling ruefully with frustration on his brow. "I meant that either man appears so taken that he may well soon offer marriage to you."

"I know what you meant."

"You make this difficult."

"Do I?" She let fly her anxiety over her need to find a good man to marry soon. "You cannot imagine how difficult it is to be a woman who must have money to marry, to marry in order to eat, to be counted as a citizen, to have a bank account, to be a legal entity to a solicitor. You cannot imagine how difficult it is to put yourself on display like a hat in a milliner's shop. To pour tea, to dress trussed up like a Christmas hen, to dance until your feet fall off, to engage in mealy discussions of weather, Prince George's finery, and the latest crop of persimmons. To long for a ripping argument about why half of Wellington's victorious army sit in the streets, begging for coin to buy bread. Or how children run vagrant because their mothers sit upstairs servicing a man and emptying a bottle of gin." She'd made a scene and with him, of all people. Tomorrow she might regret confronting him. But at the moment, triumph consumed her. "I regret the outburst. Forgive me. I must go."

"Don't leave me." He reached for her hand.

In the crowded room, if anyone noticed, she searched his repentant brown eyes for the truth in his soul.

"I do apologize, my darling, Addy. Please tell me what you want in a husband."

A man who loves me for who I truly am and not the empty-headed diamond he assumes appears before him. "A man who sees those elements that can make him truly happy. A man who works according to his skills and with his resources to build a sound living for himself and his family. I have met rakes, gamblers, men who take from others their money, their daughters, their possessions. I want an honest man who will work to create a good life for his family and himself."

He sank against the back of his chair.

She had surprised him with her fervor. Good. She'd do more. "I've met men who are greedy, miserly, taking...no, robbing other men of what they cannot earn for themselves. I want a man who has no time or interest to traffic in such crimes against another. I want a man with ethics. And yes, one with morals, too."

He appeared as enchanted as startled. "You ask a lot of a man."

She sniffed. "A husband will ask much of me."

"You wish to respect your husband. A good goal."

"He will be able to respect me. The trade is even."

Gyles nodded. "And fair."

She tugged at his hand.

"No. Please sit with me."

She longed for peace with him. "I don't want to argue. Not with you."

"Addy, I am so taken with you. You are filled with the joy of life, and yet you have known sorrow, death, a few nefarious men who have not made the best impression on your good heart. Yet you are so young."

She could not decide if that were an insult or a compliment. "I am twenty! Soon to be—"

He gave her a lopsided grin. "Twenty-one."

Soothed, she pressed her lips together and rolled her eyes at him. "Terribly old."

"But sweet and untarnished by time or circumstance."

"I have chinks in my armor, sir."

"Not large ones, my darling. Not like many young women. Or men. You are enthusiastic, positive. Out in the world to enjoy it and contribute your talents."

"I have faults. I am too proud and too determined."

"Pride in who you are is no crime," he said.

"Pride in my looks? Assets that God gave me, but none I ever worked for?"

He lifted his hand and moved as if he would thread his fingers through her hair. But in the crowded room, he took note of his surroundings and lowered his arm. "You are lovely, sweetheart. And dash it, you are rather naive about its effect on men. You'll outgrow that."

She winced. "You think so?"

"I do." He laughed.

"When?"

"As soon as you see that one man you want loves the beauty of your soul. You are too circumspect about your looks to be repulsively vain."

"I am thankful for that, too." She laughed, full to the brim with euphoria at his enchanting declarations. "While you, sir, are so devastatingly handsome."

He gave a little yelp. "You are kind to an old man."

"How old?" she asked, half dare and half tease.

"Thirty-three. Do I look aged to you?"

"No. But you are...may I say, more worldly than I?"

"I hope not irredeemably so, Addy, for that would never match with you."

"I agree. But if you see yourself too dulled by life's storms, I hope I might I lure you from the despair of it?"

"I welcome it."

"Good!" She grinned. "I accept the challenge. But it is a small one, Gyles. Smaller, dare I say, than you think. What I mean is that you do not show the world the fullness of your suffering. You have coped with that. Successfully, I think, save for your headaches. But how?"

He inhaled and set his jaw. "A long story, my darling."

"Tell me all of it. Please."

He took his time to begin. "When I was your age, I had gone to France on holiday. Encouraged by the peace between that country and Britain, I wished to do part of a grand tour that I had delayed because of Napoleon's wars. I had visited the chateaux of the Loire and the great cathedrals of Rheims and Aix when Napoleon canceled the Treaty of Amiens without warning. I hurried to pack and ride to the coast, but I was caught in Calais. We were put in chains and marched east to the Citadel of Verdun. Hungry, cold, our fine clothes frayed to rags, we feared each day for tomorrow. We were put away in one of France's oldest dungeons. It was no way to spend one's youth. I endured for more than two years. Later, with my friend Martindale and his father's help, I escaped. I did not get far but joined a renegade band to spy on the French."

"Dear Gyles," she said, longing to kiss away his remembered

horror, "how did you survive with your smile intact?"

"I ponder that. In truth? I do not know. Time heals." He picked up her hand once more, and ignoring all in the room, he brought it to his lips. "But today, with you, I think you heal me."

Her heart swelled with love for him. "Gyles, you are the finest man—"

"Ah, that I may have the chance to prove it you."

Her whole body flared with the heat of desire for him. "I want more than your lips on my hand."

His beguiling eyes danced a merry jig. "Tell me all you want of me."

"Your hands on my heart."

He smiled in such a slow seductive way that her belly quivered with need. "Your heart against mine."

"Your skin on mine."

"In a bed with candles burning."

She caught her breath. "Or in a garden with the sun blazing."

"Upon your glorious body."

Her heart stopped. "And you'd never leave me."

He shook his head. "I'd ensure you would never want to go."

She leaned closer to him, his cologne a heady lure, his lips a ripe temptation. "I don't want you to go now."

He swallowed loudly, then shot to his feet. "I must now, before I sweep you away with me."

She rose and, standing so close, she realized for the first time that the top of her head reached only to his chin. She felt so protected by him. No man had ever been her bulwark against the unknown of tomorrow. "I would love to be swept away by you."

He laughed so deeply in his throat that she felt the vibrations to her toes. "You tempt me to abduct you this minute. But I have a few things to do before we speak again. Give me time?"

She was bursting to have him now. To have him kiss her, caress her, take her away with him. "I will."

"I vow, Addy, no one else may ever have you."

"Nor you, sir. No lovers, old or new." Her pride and peace of mind demanded it of him.

"None but each other. Good day to you, my darling. I will see you tomorrow, and we will speak of this again."

"I cannot wait."

"Nor I," he said, kissed her hand, and, as if torn from her by an invisible rope, he marched away.

Chapter Five

GYLES'S HEAD SWAM with visions of Addy naked on a rich carpet before a blazing fire as he took his seat in the Banqueting Room of Prince George's sprawling Pavilion that evening. His Royal Highness gave a dinner party for his house guests and close friends—and Gyles criticized himself that he had agreed to spend hours in this tedious company.

Twenty-eight sat down, men interspersed with women, side by side at one long rectangular table. Heaped with every sort of dish from English silversmiths, Manchu porcelain china, and Irish crystal, the table groaned with endless delicacies. Above the guests' heads hung an immense iron Chinese dragon who held in his claws a giant crystal chandelier. The creature looked so lifelike, Gyles feared the monster would swoop down and gobble the food off his plate. But one look up at the sparkling glass, and Gyles saw the first flashes of a headache.

He squeezed shut his eyes and ground his teeth. With a vow to get through this dinner, he set his purpose to enjoy the evening as best he could—and speed it to its end.

Among those here were courtiers or hangers-on like Gyles's father, who gave homage and took favors from the Regent. The women in attendance, young and old, were favored by their ability to navigate the upper reaches of society, like his mother or those who flaunted every rule of man and heaven. The lady who sat to Gyles's right was one such creature, who boldly reached beneath the table linen to find his cock and cup it. He'd removed her grasping fingers from his crotch twice during the fish course and looked forward to the end of dessert—and the last of her gropes. The lady to his left was more interested in running her stockinged foot up his calf and murmuring her hopes that he might come to her rooms "after the candles are doused."

He politely claimed a headache, which sadly was not far from the truth, and hoped both ladies spread word of his disinterest in the finer elements of life. He had them in abundance. He simply did not hold them now for anyone but Adelaide Devereaux. Her discussion with him this afternoon over tea had sparked his desire to create the sort of ethical life she declared she desired. The kind of life he suddenly needed.

His father, who sat across from him, scowled at his rejection of the lady to Gyles's right. "My son weds soon," he announced in slurred syllables, signaling the duke had imbibed too much good wine.

Gyles cast his sire a long dark glare.

But both ladies on either side of Gyles reacted. One with a titter. The other with pleasant surprise.

"I say, Heath," said the one on his right, a countess of forty with an earl reputed to always stay at home in bed with his mistress, "who is she, my dear? Do we know her?"

"I have not declared myself yet, Lady Forbish."

Damned if the woman didn't slide her hand beneath the fine table cloth and give him a squeeze that crushed his nuts. "Perhaps you'd like to savor a few more varieties before you settle to one kind of dish, eh?"

He set his teeth. Removed her hand, too. "I've finished with sampling."

"No, he hasn't, Lady Forbish," said his father with stiff-lipped spite. "The one he favors carries a taint on the family line."

His father was now demeaning him in public? He'd stand for much from the sire who had always been kind to him, even if the man had not borrowed money to save him from French prison.

But Heath would not stand this criticism. "No one says that, Father."

"I do. Had proof years ago."

"Ah." Gyles would shut him up. "How does it compare to others you've known?"

Lady Forbish, shocked by the Gyles's bluntness, had ceased her search of his assets. At least one good thing had come of his sire's nastiness.

"Dunno, son. I say it's worthy here. Wouldn't you like to know, my lady, how these people've robbed hundreds of their prized possessions? They've got paintings, sculptures, even families' jewels!" His father stared at Lady Forbish with mischief in his brown eyes. Did his father know how this woman liked to fondle a man's jewels for her entertainment?

"Astonishing, Your Grace!" Lady Forbish had the good sense and courtesy to dismiss him.

"I promise more later, then." The ungracious Duke of Stonegage raised his glass in a promise.

"Do that, Papa, and you stoop to the same level as the man whose name you wish to tarnish." That was aggressive, but Gyles no longer cared if his father suffered embarrassment at this table. Gyles, tempted though he was, should not rise to leave the insulting conversation. One did not leave the table before the Regent, even if George appeared well into his own cups. But shame his father, Gyles would, if the man continued in this vein. His own discourtesy he would make amends for, always.

"The whole family is corrupt. Blood tells, my boy."

"Boy" had long been the term that could send Gyles over to a void. The word had been the one French guards used in Verdun to shame their British prisoners. Old or young received the dismissive appellation freely and often with beatings to accompany, including Gyles. Worse, his father knew the word could rouse the devil in his only son and heir.

If minutes ago he'd seen flashes from the tiny swaying crystals above his head, he now saw them flare in anger. One type of megrim was as bad as the other.

"Forgive me, my lady," Gyles said to the woman on his left. To Lady Forbish he said, "Please disregard whatever you hear from my father. I must leave at once. I find the air quite morbid."

"By your bad manners, boy, you shall not deter me!"

By yours, you cannot rule my life. Gyles had learned to think for himself in Verdun. He would not stop now.

He lifted his brow at a nearby footman. The servant rushed to his side. "Convey my apologies to His Royal Highness, as I am suddenly ill."

At that, he threw down his serviette, shot to his feet, and strode away.

ADDY ACCEPTED THE hand of the Rensfords' footman to climb the gangway to the family yacht. Head down, she picked her way along the uneven planks and fought the *frisson* of calamity that shook her to her bones. She had slept well last night, yet this morning she was shrouded in a stormy premonition of disaster. Their mother had often felt a similar cloud before a horrendous event occurred to her or a member of the family. Neither Laurel or Imogen shared this trait, and thus, Addy kept her trepidations to herself.

"You are quiet, Adelaide." Cass patted her hand as she and Laurel joined her on deck. "You do like to sail, don't you?"

Unlike poor Imogen, Addy had no such challenges with the roll and pitch of the sea. Because of Imogen's poor stomach, she had remained at home and happily waved off the other three to today's event. Lord and Lady Rensford, lights of Brighton society, hosted a select group of guests on their own vessel. The regatta today was not a race, per se, but an excuse by the Rensfords and one other family to show off their new yachts.

"I do enjoy the sea, Cass. When we were little, Grandpapa

took us to Cork, where he was a member of the Water Club. We'd sail down in his schooner for races in the summer. Not Imogen, of course. My only concern now," she said as she fingered her parasol in her failure to spot Gyles on the dock, "is the sun."

"Be sure to find your way to the ladies' saloon to sit in the shade," Cass said. "Each of us is very fair. And we have much to do these next few days. A red complexion won't help us in any way!" Cass sounded much too happy and turned her attention to the receiving line of their hosts. "Let's present ourselves. Shall we?"

As Addy and Imogen took their places beside Cass, silence fell.

Laurel caught Addy's gaze. With a glance, she led Addy to observe Cass kneading her hands. The lovely lady who had come to their rescue was a lioness of London society. Affable, accomplished, and at thirty-six still considered an Incomparable, Cassandra, Lady William Downs, had never twiddled a thumb in distress. Yet since their first night at the Exleighs' ball, Cass acted oddly. She embroidered often, though lately, her stitches were a cat's ball of dull colors. She played the pianoforte usually beautifully, yet lately, lost notes. She also daydreamed, and that had never been her practice before that fated ball.

Today, she showed a penchant to describe in abundant and repetitive detail each person in the receiving line.

Addy shrugged at Laurel, unable to divine the cause of Cass's behavior.

Other guests ahead of them chatted quietly among themselves, and Addy pouted when she still did not spot Gyles's tall form. She craned her neck to survey the dock. Alas, she spotted two men whose interest in Laurel had not pleased her oldest sister in the least.

Addy cleared her throat and nudged Laurel's elbow to direct her attention to the gangway.

Her sister took one look and raised her brows in exclamation.

The two fellows who had consumed her attention at tea yesterday, Lords Penury and Warble—as Addy had vicariously dubbed them—had not come up to the mark for Laurel's hand.

Cass, who had the latest *on dit* about everyone, had told them more as they traveled to Cowes this morning. "Lord Penhurst lost an extremely large amount at cards last week. I also have it on good authority that he is not the best manager of his little estate."

Lord Warble seemed no better.

"He's a widower twice over," Cass added with a frown.

Laurel set her teeth. Yesterday, she'd told Addy that Warble was missing quite a few of his own.

"Sad, really." Cass continued.

To which Laurel nodded.

"He's only thirty-one."

Laurel sent Addy a squinty-eyed grimace and ran a finger across her wrist. Laurel had heard that Warble's two wives died in the country soon after each lady had birthed a baby.

"But poor Warbleton needs an heir. Two daughters will not do the trick for him."

Worse, Laurel had remarked yesterday that the fellow had breathed upon her and nearly blew her over with his bad breath.

Laurel leaned close now to whisper to her, "Help me stay far away, please."

"Of course," Addy said as her gaze swept the dock. Lord Hewett and the Duke of Lonsdale emerged from their own carriages.

If fate had in store for Addy any surprises soon, one fact she knew for certain. "We'll rescue each other today."

Words, however, were weak swords against the onslaught of rivalrous men.

Lord Hewett took to Addy as soon as the yacht sailed out to sea. The currents coming through the Channel to Cowes were choppy today, and Addy made the excuse to him that she had to seek the quiet shelter of the ladies' saloon aft. Comfortable and cool there, she sat talking with two ladies when Lord Warble, of all people, insinuated himself into the group. Displeased that he occupied a coveted chair meant for a woman, Addy fumed when he brought her a glass of white wine, and in effect, shooed her two friends away.

"You are so popular, Miss Adelaide," Warble said. "No wonder with your lively manner."

She didn't like to drink on board and put the glass aside. His compliment rang an alarm in her head. What had happened to his fascination for Laurel? But then, her sister could burn a man's ears, revealing her true feelings. "Kind of you to say, sir."

"I wonder if you like children."

"Children. I do. Very much. It's my understanding you have two, sir."

"Fine little girls." He inched closer and Addy, in self-defense, sat back. Even the wind off the sea could not wipe away evidence of his lack of tooth powder. "I've hired a fine nanny and new governess for them. They live in the country, of course. London is too hectic for a child's constitution."

And what of a wife's? Is a woman's constitution too weak for the town?

"Do you like England?" he asked, much too gaily.

Oh, no. He was wooing her? How had this fellow gotten the impression that he could court Addy since Laurel did not take his bait?

"Very much, sir. I enjoyed London and would favor living there more than any rustic backwater." She had no idea where Warble had his estate, but she would never give him cause to think she'd go anywhere with him.

"How wonderful!" The devilish gleam in his grey eyes told her he lied. "I seek to make a complete family for my daughters."

"A worthy goal, my lord."

"I must do it soon."

"Really? Why is that?" Did he simply wish to have a son soon, or was he yearning to have his needs serviced?

"The two little ones pine for a woman to cuddle them."

"I'm sure they do, sir. Children need all the cuddles they can get."

"Exactly my thought, Miss Adelaide. I do wonder if I may call on you."

Direct, and foolishly so. "I doubt that, sir."

Surprised, he blinked and covered his dismay. "Do you always speak so bluntly?"

"To questions such as that, yes."

His pale eyes flashed with pride and insult. But he smiled, tight though it was. "Very well. I will make my excuses to you."

"Please."

With a satisfaction she had not felt in ages, she applauded herself for telling him the bald truth. She inhaled and sought the company of a few ladies chatting in one corner.

As she passed Cass, her cousin took her arm. "I must speak with you. In private. Tonight."

"What's wrong?" Addy caught a note of despair in Cass's statement.

"Not here. Later, dear. Do smile."

That shook her. She put on a bright face, but solitude beckoned. Anxiety won the day. Within minutes, she headed for the ladies' retiring room below.

Rushing along the deck to the stairs, she felt her premonition of disaster rise with a strong wind. Gyles, for whatever reason, had not appeared. Instinct said what was amiss was a question of his attraction to her, and she wished she could simply jump in the sea and swim home.

She rushed down, putting on a brave front. Hearing voices, she thrust open the first door. The room, however, offered no retreat. It contained one small desk, two chairs, and a round flat table. Upon it were two people who never heard her turn the knob nor noticed that they were far too well observed.

Addy rushed up the stairs.

"Forgive me, Your Grace," Addy appeared at Laurel's side

and intruded on her conversation with the Duke of Lonsdale. "I must have my sister's help. Thank you so much."

She tugged Laurel across the deck toward the steps below. "Lower cabin for us," she explained.

"Thank God. I tried to escape him to no end!"

"Imagine what our lives would be like if we had a fortune!" Addy groused.

Laurel burst out laughing. "And you wanted more than the two thousand!"

"Not anymore. I'd like to keep my virginity for my wedding night...and at this rate..." Addy hissed as she wound her arm in her sister's and rushed her down the tiny hall. "Listen to me. We have a problem."

"Too many men we dislike?" She hiccupped. Then clapped a hand over her mouth. "Sorry. Too much wine."

"Right. Don't drink anymore."

"I won't."

"Good."

"What's our problem?"

Addy leaned into Laurel's ear and said, "Cass."

"I don't..."

Addy pointed her forefinger toward the door in question. "Two people who amuse themselves together."

Laurel's large jade eyes twinkled. "What's wrong with that?"

"Are you foxed?"

Laurel hiccupped once more. "I could be."

Frowning, Addy said, "Straighten up."

"You never get angry. What is the matter?"

"You're inebriated, and I need you."

She put two fingers across her lips. "For what?"

Addy looked down the hall and wondered if she was searching for an answer or a bucket of ice water to throw over her tipsy sister. "Cass is in there," she ground out. "With a man."

Laurel's mouth dropped open.

"Yes," Addy hissed. "Atop a table."

Her jaw fell further.

"Her bodice is down."

Laurel gulped.

"And she must be saved."

Laurel blinked, showing Addy at that moment that her sister did not require ice water. "Now."

"Exactly." Addy straightened her shoulders.

"Well? Ideas?" Laurel asked, her focus on said door.

Addy flinched. "Scream 'fire'? Jump overboard?"

Laurel tipped her head to one side. "Garrr. We knock!"

Addy wrinkled her nose. "We save her before someone *else* interrupts them."

"Ha!" Laurel burped. "Sorry. Do it."

Addy rapped. Loudly.

They each pressed an ear to the polished wood. A few groans and a grumble rent the air.

Addy knocked once more. Harder.

At that unfortunate moment, Lord Hewett stumbled his way down the steps, presumably headed for the men's convenience. "Have you a problem, ladies?" He smiled crookedly, then licked his lips, in no small measure full of spirits himself.

"We are well." Laurel nodded and put a thumb up to motion toward the door in question. "Just waiting for a friend."

Hewett made a similar motion with his own thumb. All right for him, then, as he pushed open the door he wanted and disappeared.

Addy winced. "He can stay in there the rest of the afternoon, for all I care."

"Shhh. Here is—"

The door swished open, and the man who stood before them was the giant creature whom much of Brighton heralded, one of Wellington's greatest war heroes. He wore his regimentals, and at the moment, he wore them rather poorly, his scarlet coat unbuttoned and one medal askew upon his broad beribboned chest.

Addy recognized him, having met him at Exleighs' ball the other night.

"Ladies," said Colonel Lord Magnus Augustus Welles of the Third Regiment of Foot in acknowledgment and gave a courteous bow. He ran two meaty hands into the long golden locks of his hair. "The cousins, I see. Good of you to find us."

He paused, deigned to bless them with a half-smile, and turned to speak to Cass, who remained hidden behind the half-opened door. "Breathe, my darling. You're saved."

He swung wide the door to reveal their cousin, as stunned as a girl who'd just been caught eating candy. Her blue eyes were limpid, her cheeks aflame, her lips swollen from kisses. Her skirts rumpled.

Welles pulled his coat to, then threw a wink to the woman he'd ravished.

Addy and Laurel rushed inside and shut the door. They did not ask; they did not comment, nor would they ever. They went to work to straighten their cousin's gown and pin her hair so that minutes later, the three emerged and rejoined the party on deck.

Cass regained her aplomb.

Laurel steered clear of all men—and wine.

Addy was left to toss in her own turmoil, trying to remain jovial, yet questioning what had happened to Gyles that he had not come today. She feared, too, that the information Cass wanted to impart held the disastrous news her premonition foretold. More, she worried that with his withdrawal, she'd lost her chance for the same magic she'd glimpsed on Cass's face when they pushed wide that tiny room's door.

As dusk fell, she climbed into their carriage with Cass and Laurel. The horses made their way back home to Brighton, and all three inside the coach nestled into their corner squabs and sighed.

Laurel crossed her arms, closed her eyes, and soon snored.

Cass stirred and caught Addy's gaze. "Rumors of your grandfather's actions go round. The one who has stirred them is the

Duke of Stonegage."

Addy shivered and pulled her pelisse close up about her chin. Hot tears stung her eyes. *Why did women have to be judged by the men in their family? Could not a woman establish a reputation for herself? All the more reason to turn my skill with healing herbs and potions into a useful practice.*

"We'll be discreet about this," Cass murmured. "I will ensure the town knows how pristine your backgrounds are."

Cass had been so helpful in all their turmoils. "I trust you. Do what you think is appropriate."

Addy crossed her arms and huddled into herself. Her premonition of disaster had blossomed like an evil flower. But she hated that her grandfather's profession had caught up with her and her sisters. She had to draw the only conclusion. Stonegage had talked to his son and persuaded him to stay away.

Chapter Six

THAT NIGHT, ADDY crept from her bed and ran down the hall to Imogen's room. As she opened the door, she saw by the light of the moon that her sister sat up, wide awake.

"May I talk to you?"

"Of course." Imogen plumped her pillows behind her and patted the bed for Addy to join her. They'd often sat like this, starry-eyed and needing each other's company.

"Did you enjoy your day?" Imogen asked as she tucked her covers up around Addy's legs. The three had arrived so late from Cowes that none of them had visited to share details of the day.

"Pleasant. However, Gyles did not appear."

"'Gyles' is it now? Not even Heath?"

Addy shrugged. "The familiarity was a good sign. Now, we have a problem."

"Why? Because he did not attend? I wouldn't put stock in so little a thing. He's lodging at Prinny's, you know. I doubt they can hie off at any time without old George getting in a snit."

"Yes. But there is more. Much more, and I hoped you would tell me what you know."

Imogen's eyes went wide. "Darling Addy, I have no idea why your beau would not go sailing today."

"No, no. Not why he would not sail today. But worse. You see, rumor has reached Cass that Gyles's father has stirred old tales of Grandpapa."

Imogen stared into her eyes, caught like a deer down the sight of a hunter. "Oh."

"Yes. That."

"You know we do not speak of it."

Addy took Imogen's hand and squeezed. "But we must. The house in Dublin is shuttered. By Grandpapa's orders, it will go up for sale as soon as the estate manager empties it."

"The man has many problems with that," Imogen said.

"And we know why, don't we?"

"Oh, Addy!" Imogen swept a hand through her long golden hair, shining white in the moonlight. "It will do us no good to know. Grandpapa is dead."

"You think it is reasonable to have the entire contents sold and for us to reap the profits?"

"No. Not completely. But that part of Grandpapa's last will we were never told about. Not officially."

"But it's what we suspect." Addy had an idea why that was so. But to call it into question was to challenge the work of their oldest sister, Laurel. The last person to work on Grandfather's will was Laurel. She was the one who took care of their grandfather's books and receipts. For the last two years of his life, Laurel managed it all. And at his death, Laurel had delivered the will, signed and sealed, to the estate managers. The short description ordering the sale of the house and its contents was the last item written in the will.

"And you don't want to challenge Laurel's work on Grandpapa's will, do you?"

Imogen rolled a shoulder. "No."

Addy noted the lack of an explanation. That verified her own suspicion that Imogen and Laurel kept secrets from her. They always had. Laurel, older by eight minutes than Imogen, and Imogen older than Addy by four hours and eight minutes, had always played the parts of big sisters. They were triplets, but to see how the oldest two acted toward Addy, one would think they were years older.

Very well, she'd let that slide in favor of what she could learn and could change. "Is there a listing of the art?"

"A listing? Dear God." Imogen fell back against the pillows. "I hope not."

"We have to make some sense of it. How can you sell what you do not know you own?"

"Own?" Imogen shook her head. "I do not know if we *own* any of it."

So disturbed by the prospect, Addy jumped from the bed and paced. "What do you call it then? Borrowing?"

"Of course not, but how do we know the provenance of any item that's there?"

"Provenance? We must know something!" Addy whirled around to face her sister, undone by the enormity of the problem. "When I saw it, I was…. I don't know…fourteen…fifteen…there were hundreds of paintings. Dozens of sculptures. I was struck like lightning at how much stood there."

"I know," Imogen said, hanging her head in a sorrowful nod. "I could not believe what was behind that false wall. I'd never noticed the false door until it stood open one morning. He'd forgotten to close it when he was drunk. He was in his cups and opened the hidden door to go pet them, of all things. When I saw the room chock full of treasures the first time, I think I was ten years old. Perhaps older. It knocked me to my bum. I stood, like a ninny, with my mouth open, and then I walked through long rows of silver and gilded frames. Portraits of kings and queens stared back at me. Pirates grinned from their decks. Young children posed with their spaniels. Landscapes of Shropshire and China, and bowls of apples and bananas lay at my feet. My jaw dropped. I couldn't fathom where he'd gotten all that or how or why. But then…he took me by the hand and led me away and locked the false door behind me."

Addy sighed. "So he was indeed the greatest fencer in Ireland."

"He was."

"And our problem now is how to return these items to their proper owners."

"And how to do it quietly so that no one blames us for possessing them."

"Or continues to talk about Grandpapa or us." Suddenly chilled, Addy secured her robe high up around her throat. "Laurel won't help us on this, will she?"

Imogen shook her head. "We mustn't ask her. There is a reason..."

Imogen's words hung in the air like a sword.

Addy caught back her horror. "You won't tell me, will you?"

Imogen frowned. "I can't. She...she refuses to speak of what she did for Grandpapa at the end."

Addy inhaled, ready to fight for a proper disposition of all the art. "We must write to the estate manager and tell him to keep us informed of the disposition of each piece."

Imogen rolled her shoulders, unconvinced. "I must think if we can find a way to break this to Laurel..."

"We must."

Her sister nodded, not quite in agreement, but close.

At the door, Addy paused with her hand to the latch. "Are there works by any famous artists whom you and I have heard of?"

"Oh, yes. Hans Holbein. Rembrandt. A sketch by Da Vinci."

The enormity of this problem hit her like a rock. Her eyes closed. She'd heard enough. "Thank you for telling me."

"We are the three Devereaux girls. And we will find happiness despite this."

Addy nodded. She would work to make it so, whatever the cost.

"MY LORD?" THE estate agent hurried toward Gyles and his two friends, who stood grinning at each other like fools in the front parlor.

After moving out of the Pavilion at dawn this morning, Gyles had collected his friends Viscount Grey and Captain Fitzroy at Grey's house on the Steine, then roused the rental agent from his office on the Marine Parade at nine o'clock this morning. The man had shown him two other houses today, but this one was no dreary Dutch clinker. With a white stucco exterior complemented by two bays of tall Venetian windows, the manse had precisely the flair of the architect Robert Adams.

The expansive first floor sported two salons—one for receiving, one for family—a dining room with table and chairs to seat twelve, ample kitchen below with alcoves for staff to sleep nearby, servants' dining room, larders, plate room, a wine cellar, kitchen garden, and privy. Three family bedrooms lay above with a master suite that pleased a man of Gyles's stature and marital ambitions. On the topmost floor, five servants' rooms, three for one person each, two for two. Enough to run a small household for an indefinite period of time. Plus, a skeleton staff of butler and footman were always on duty at payment by the owner, the Earl of Penderyn. That the house also came with fashionable furniture, linens, silver, and china solved Gyles need for quick occupancy.

What sold it for him, more so, was the tiny Italianate garden to the rear, where a profusion of flowering bushes and plants gave a fragrance to the sea breeze. Addy would adore the place.

"Lord Heath? You approve, sir?"

"I do. I'll take it for the Season until at least October, perhaps longer. I will notify you. I have no valet here. He remained at my house in London. I'll bring him later. But I'd appreciate it if you provided Penderyn's regular staff for me. If they are not at call, then hire from the local servants' registry."

"I can, sir."

"Excellent. A fine cook, too, mind you." Addy enjoyed a fine meal.

"Absolutely."

Gyles nodded, pleased with his success. "To start as soon as possible. When might that be?"

"Three to four days, sir." The agent fairly floated in the air with Gyles's consent.

Gyles swung toward two gentlemen who stood, surveying the blue and gold salon with as much glee as if they were renting it for themselves. "What do you think, my friends?"

Hadley Sherborne, Viscount Grey, uncrossed his arms and chuckled. "Fast work."

"Fine work," said Captain Fitzroy, who, like Grey, had attended Eton with Gyles long ago. "You'll impress the lady with your choices."

"Necessary." He concluded, so pleased with himself.

THE VERY IDEA of attending church that Sunday morning stole Addy's appetite. She'd spent the night punching her pillows, gutted by Gyles's loss and the news that she and her sisters were about to pay a horrid price for the notoriety of their grandfather's pastime. She'd find no comfort in hearing any pious prelate preach about forgiveness. All that pontificating only made her cry. And she hated to cry.

So it was that all the others went out, leaving her to sit alone in the little yellow dining room. There, as she stewed about Gyles's absence and his cockish reputation, she bemoaned the pile of art their Grandpapa had stashed in his long false gallery. All that to say nothing about her fear that rumors of Cass's liaison with that colonel might explode.

Richards, their jolly butler, puttered around her. "Might I remove the servers from the sideboard, Miss?"

"Indeed, you may, Richards. I'll have just my tea."

He cocked a bushy eyebrow. "Cook worries that you did not

partake of her biscuits and eggs this morning, Miss Adelaide. She asks if she can tempt you with a bit, say, of yesterday's strawberry pie?" He gazed at her with a toothy grin. "You have such a robust appetite."

She brightened at that offer. Pie of any type always filled her head with pleasures of summer. "I do, that's true. Thank her, Richards. I'll enjoy a small piece."

"Excellent!" He rushed off.

She drummed her fingers on the tablecloth. She probably should have gone to church. The quiet house encouraged brooding—and she rejected that. She liked a spirited household, full of her sisters, her grandfather, and his old butler who reminded her of Richards. She also missed the dogs of the family. Big hairy bouncing Irish hounds with long snouts, slobbering into her hands and giving as good as they got in affection.

Richards arrived with her pie, and she made quick work of it.

Licking her lips, she inhaled, then stood and resolved to do what must be done.

Build a life for herself that had nothing to do with Grandpapa or his past. If Gyles no longer found her suitable because of her family, she would not accept any other man. Her heart ached at that, but she would not attempt to make him love her if her bloodline was more important to him than her character.

She had an interest in herbs and such, and as long as she learned enough not to kill anyone, she'd save a few people from illness. No time like the present to pursue her goal.

"MADEMOISELLE ADELAIDE, I do not like this." Fifi scowled at the ramshackle condition of the shops in this particular lane. "*Gitans! Dangereuse, ma cherie.*"

This far south end of the Lanes was reserved for wanderers. Addy did not flinch from any association with them. She'd known a family who'd camped on the coast in Waterford, and from them, she learned how to make a mint tea that cured Grandpapa of his winter sore throats. "They are people with special talents, Fifi. I have need of an acquaintance with them." *While I am in Brighton, I might well prepare myself to have a skill that will enrich my life more than money. Or a man.*

"No good, I say. No good." Fifi's large grey eyes showed white at the edges. She pulled the collar of her pelisse up around her shoulders.

"Wait here, Fifi." Addy pointed to the rough wooden bench in front of the fortune teller's shop. "Nothing will happen to me. I just have a few questions of the woman in here. I'll be out shortly."

"*Oui, allez!*"

Addy pushed open the blood-red door, and the creak of the hinges hurt her ears. She marched inside. "Hello?! Hello?" She called to the person whose name appeared on the shop door. "*Madam Alain?*"

She repeated the call twice before she heard a groan from the far back of the shop and footsteps, hard and heavy, advance toward the front. With a swish of hundreds of hanging chains of colorful beads, a woman appeared. With wildly wavy black hair and puffy coal-rimmed eyes, she wrapped a vibrant red and purple knit shawl around her copious bosom and scrutinized Addy. "I do not rid town ladies of unwanted babies."

"Oh, I—"

"And I don't prepare poisons for husbands who cheat."

"No, I—"

"I don't make doses to make your man, as you say, priapic."

A prick. Addy knew the meaning of *that*. "I have no idea what *priapric* means, but I'll ask you that later."

Cursing in her own bright language, the woman narrowed her gaze on Addy and, with a decided squint of her luminous eyes, tried to give her a bit of a start. But Addy held her ground. She'd met a pirate on the coast of Waterford when she was twelve, and no one had scared her since.

He'd had one eye, a dirty black patch, and wielded one long scary dagger. After he saw she held a jagged rotten tree limb as her defense, he buckled in laughter and settled in to tell her his tales of sailing the Caribbean and running men out of Africa. For weeks, she visited him on the shore, and he told her ribald jokes whose meaning, by implication, had taught her much of men and intercourse. They'd become friends until one day, weeks later, without a word, he disappeared, and she mourned his loss.

By contrast, this lady was not as frightening as she wished to appear. Still, she must have harbored hope of it and advanced on Addy. "You are who, and why are you here?"

This grumpy fortune-teller has not had her morning tea. "I've heard from Mister Alworth that you know your medicinals."

"My what?"

So we must speak in real terms. "Herbs. Plants. Insects. Animals. Healing foods."

"You do not wish to kill someone?"

"No."

The lady put one hand on her hip and gestured toward Addy's stomach. "You have no babe in your belly?"

"Someday, I hope so. But I have no man either. Not yet." *Maybe never if I cannot conjure the same euphoria when I'm with someone other than Gyles. And if Gyles does not want me now...*

"A virgin?" Madam Alain leaned toward her with menace framing her jaw.

She had to be the most suspicious person Addy had ever met. "I am."

"You flow regular?"

"I do."

"She will have four fine sons," came a guttural voice somewhere in the depths of the shop behind Madam Alain.

"I will?" *This was definitely the best idea to come here.* "Are you sure?"

"Big. Healthy," came the response from the same unseen

older woman who had a voice made of the leather of a bass drum. "No girls."

"Oh, good!" Addy clasped her hands together, tingling at the idea of such a large strapping family, though she did sorrow that she'd have no little girl to fuss over.

Madam Alain tipped her head toward the door. "Take your prediction and go."

"Oh, no! I don't want to. I mean, I did not come for news of my future."

The woman strolled forward and peered at her. But now, she looked not at Addy's exterior but down, far down, into her soul. "Why did you say you came here?"

"I hope you will teach me about healing people of sicknesses. I know a few remedies. A midwife in my small town would sit with me each Sunday morning while others in the family went to church." Addy licked her lips, seeing boredom on the face of this startlingly handsome woman. "I want to learn what you know. Good remedies to make people healthy."

"When you learn how to heal, you also learn how to kill."

This lady was no easy mark. "I understand, Madam."

"She cannot kill, Drusinda," came the voice from the back room.

"You have not seen her, Marska," replied Drusinda with a harsh examination of Addy's steady blue eyes.

So many had peered at Addy in that same intensity. Men in desire. Women in envy. Children in shock or reverence. She did not move but let the woman look her fill.

"I hear her," was the gravelly voiced woman's reply. "I smell her intent. I see her spirit."

Drusinda pulled her shawl higher and pointed toward two chairs. "Sit."

Chapter Seven

T HE NEXT EVENING at the Carstairs' musicale, Addy rushed into the brilliant red salon behind her sisters, and Cass and swore she'd find an interesting man here tonight. One she might even indulge in the opportunity to kiss her. Or rather, she to test him for his "bliss factor." Beauty, as she had always known firsthand, should never be a girl's only drawing card. One had to have daring at the least, a pointed desire to taste as many men as possible before the choice was put upon one. Too bad her desire to kiss as many men as appealed to her had vanished at the sight of magnificent Gyles.

Addy resigned herself to a new and potent search for a reasonably attractive and jovial man. Her luck held when she was introduced before dinner to a young cavalryman, Captain Reginald Fitzroy. Handsome in a sharp, dark, and forbidding way, he endeared himself to her with his broad smiles and dangerous green eyes. Their hostess indicated the party was soon to go into the dining room when who should appear but Gyles.

"Heath" or "my lord" to her from now on.

Addy's heart stopped at how madly he searched the room, ignoring all, even the hostess. Then he halted, locking his brown eyes on hers. She swung away from his lure, his mouth-watering might in formal black frock coat, trousers, and polished shoes. Yet his essence lived in her reverie. His highly starched stock had leant luster to his fine complexion, burnished by his ruby satin waistcoat and sunlight that he'd obviously enjoyed somewhere other than the Cowes regatta.

She busied herself talking to someone about some little thing but perceived he worked his way through a few remarks to his host and hostess. He even headed Addy's way when Lady Carstairs indicated they were ready for dinner. Each guest filed up according to their station. Addy thrilled to find herself seated, a la the Prince Regent's mixed-method, next to a moody fellow, a curate in a parish west of Brighton, and to her right, the very wicked-looking cavalryman, Fitzroy.

Heath had assumed his place four down the long table. Opposite her but within sight, he took long notice of her, smiled, and nodded with no hint of his feelings. While he was seated with an older lady to his left and Cass to his right, he could not for the next hour and a half take his gaze from Addy or her dashing companion to her right.

Addy, as a result, ate her dinner with relish.

Heath appeared to play with his food.

Good. Let him.

⇒⇒⇒⫸⫷⫷⫷

As THE GUESTS adjourned to the music room, Gyles made his way toward Addy, through the throng of men. The curate who'd sat to one side of her at dinner—was Fellowes his name?—had seemed too animated to be a curate. Flirting with her, the rascal. And failing. Were not curates asexual creatures?

Fitz, who had sat to her right, stayed there. Looking all the crack, bright and shining in his red and gold regimentals, Fitz— the coy dog—was eyeing Gyles as he approached.

He was about to gain on them when Fitz handed her a glass of champagne. One, in fact, which she definitely did not need as much as the one in his own hand intended for her.

Curse it. He discarded the flute of bubbly and went for the object of his desire. Fitz would give over. Or should.

"Good evening, Miss Adelaide. Fitzroy. I say, you do look stunning in that ivory." *You are a goddess in anything. Nothing, however, would be my preference.*

Addy regarded him cool as ice. "We were just discussing Napoleon's new home in the south of the Atlantic Ocean. Captain Fitzroy, I did not know you two were acquainted." She looked upon that man with more dismay than she ever had Gyles.

"We are," Fitz replied with a wink at Gyles.

"Old school chums," Gyles said. "To your topic, though, my experience with Bony was that he and his henchmen are wily men, grasping always for power. In my opinion, the South Pole is not far enough away to neutralize him."

Fitzroy spoke up. "We shall keep the little emperor holed up in the desolate place until his death. And that is the end of our worries and our wars. But then, Heath, I saw only the Frenchman's might on the field. You knew of him as a wily diplomat."

Gyles worked at hiding the smile that curled his mouth. Fitz was trying to gild his lily for him in front of the lady? "True. After I escaped Verdun, I served for a few years with an espionage group north of Reims."

"Dangerous work, sir!" Fitzroy said and raised his glass.

"Enough! The two of you!" Addy let out a laugh.

Fitz wiggled his brows. "I see my efforts are not necessary here! Excuse me, Gyles. Miss." And off he went.

"Addy, I wish to talk with you."

"Why?"

"Please join me for a turn on the terrace."

But Lady Carstairs called for everyone's attention as she stood before the pianoforte and welcomed her guests to the treat of the first soloist of the evening. Addy put down her glass of champagne and went to stand near the hostess.

SHE'D VOLUNTEERED HER singing. Not the best, she admitted. But better than many. As long as she was able to choose the ditty—and she had informed Lady Carstairs of her song well before dinner—she'd perform suitably. Initially, she'd volunteered to take her mind from the fact that Gyles had not appeared at this party. Perhaps she'd even sing to attract new beaux. But no matter Gyles's appearance here and his invitation to the terrace, she'd press on as she always did in any endeavor. Even if she proved not the most proficient at music, she always tried to be better at anything she tried. That was worth much, especially to her. After all, a girl had to be more than her looks.

Across the room, she saw Imogen startle at her introduction. Her sisters called her tone-deaf. Her mother had often been embarrassed. *A cat*, Grandpapa had said, *sounds better, dear heart.* Perhaps so, but she'd been working at improvement when they weren't around. Off to the seamstress or the milliner they'd gone and left her with the temptation of the piano and a way to perfect her singing. Like a Lorelei, she'd try it. Had to. What else was there in life but to try and improve, eh?

As she inhaled and clasped her hands together like a Drury Lane performer, Addy called on her serenity and just then saw her courage work its magic. Gyles arched his brows in approval, and she couldn't help that her heart took wing.

Caterwaul, she would not.

She cleared her throat, forgot about the crowd sitting before her with much-too-saccharine smiles, and proceeded. She began in slow, middle ranges of an Irish country song. A tale of a young lass who discovered love with an English soldier, the ditty spoke of her longing for his return. When at last he did arrive years later to claim her, he had been brutally wounded in war, and he asked if she might still love him. Of course she did. She had waited for her true love, you see. Addy adored the tale, and to her delight, she came to the end of it with the audience gleefully applauding her. She curtsied and grinned into Gyles's eyes as he maneuvered himself close beside her, outpacing even the very-eager curate, Mister Fellowes.

"Come talk with me, please, Addy." Gyles led her toward the chairs at the back of the room but did not sit. Taking her hand in his, he bent over her as he spoke and sounded so appealing that she could not deny him.

Glancing around the room, she searched for Cass but did not see her. Nor did she notice that handsome giant in regimentals who had been secluded with her cousin in the cabin Saturday on the Rensfords' yacht. Cass might not approve of Addy removing herself for a private conversation, even to the well-occupied terrace. But if Addy could not find her because Cass, herself, was too busy kissing a man, who was Addy to deny herself the chance to speak with the man who, with a word, could break her heart again?

She nodded in agreement.

When they stood just outside the terrace doors, and the starlit night enveloped her with false hope he might still want her, he grasped both her hands. "I wanted to apologize for not seeing you in Cowes."

She lifted a shoulder. She could lie and say there was no need for that, but still, her pride was pricked that he'd not come to Cowes. "You might send your apologies to the Rensfords, sir."

His features fell. "Am I now 'sir' to you? Terrible that. I thought we had progressed nicely to our given names."

"We might revert to that." She teetered on a precipice, ready to fall for him so easily.

"I have a good reason for not attending the Rensfords' party."

She waited. But he struggled with an explanation. "Very well. I know a man has business matters to pursue."

"Indeed, I do. And it concerns you, Addy."

She arched her brows. "Should you tell me?"

"I wish to, yes. You see, someone told me that in Dublin and London, you recently took to kissing any man who intrigued you."

"Gossips!" She could deny it, but why? She was not a liar. Not even about her...hmm...extraordinary behavior. No Devereaux girl was a liar. Such a characteristic did help to save the family honor. Or so they had all agreed years ago. "Why listen to them?"

He leaned in closer to put his mouth near her ear and whisper, "Anything anyone has to say about you concerns me. I listen but do not believe. Not unless you confirm. Do you kiss those who appeal to you?"

"I did. Before I met you. Not since." *What good did my restraint do me?*

"The very thing I wanted to hear." He pulled her so divinely close, her nipples blossomed against his chest.

She wanted to melt against him. A swift glance told her others on the terrace had seemed to float inside. How many were left, she did not pause to count. His voice, his words, the very fragrance of his cologne wafted around her like a magic mist. She put a palm to his broad warm chest and felt his pounding heartbeat. He crushed her nearer, and she nestled her hips against his. She slid her arms around his shoulders. Pressed against him like this, she knew the length of his cock. Her body gushed with liquid heat, and she yearned to have him fill the empty caverns of her body.

"No one is left here but us, my darling woman." He cupped her chin and raised her face to look at him. "This man would very much like to kiss you the way he's yearned to do since he first saw you days ago. Don't you yearn to kiss me, my darling?"

Enough of this blarney! She drove her hands up his shoulders and grabbed two handfuls of his downy hair. "Yes, for heaven's sake! Kiss me."

Now Addy had kissed...perhaps, five men. Flights to the moon? No, none were. But each was an education. Some men kissed like little birds, pecking at a girl's mouth. Some dove in as if they were conquering heroes, but claimed her like a sword, heavy on the thrust and hard on the grasp. Other men kissed with wet lips or dry ones. As if they sampled fish. But Gyles's opened a new world of exploration.

His lips seared hers, pressing hers open, invading her mouth with his smooth, fast tongue and sweeping away all she'd learned from others. This was no coy tasting of her lips. No dip into the cavern of her mouth. This was a lover's claim, a slow enchantment of her reason and her decorum. Had she ever thought that a woman could be undone by a meeting of lips, she understood now how she could be driven witless. So as he drew away, her vision grew cloudy. Her heart pounded like a little bird's. Her knees wobbled.

She stood, only with the help of his arms. "That was...spectacular."

He was as breathless as she. "I want you. Like this. Against me. Part of me."

His frank appeal undid her. She swept her palm down his massive ribs along his groin to cup his heavy length. "I could want you, too. Always. Like this."

He groaned and rained kisses down her throat and along the bodice of her gown.

She arched up, straining to have more.

"Adelaide Devereaux," he breathed and, with his teeth, took down her gown and sucked her aching nipple into his hot mouth. To be savored by him was paradise.

She gasped, stroking his iron-hard member. "I've never wanted any man as I want you."

His answer came as he laved her nipple and took down the other side of her bodice to suckle her other breast. "You are so beautiful. Addy, I promise I could make you very happy."

"Do it," she pleaded. "Do it now."

He complied as he lifted her, taking her to the shadows where he set her upon the stone balustrade. He stepped between her thighs and pushed up one side of her skirts. "Lovely woman." He brushed his palm up her bare calf and her thigh to her pulsing center, where he set his fingers stroking her intimate flesh. "Open for me."

She had no mind to refuse but let him in. He pressed two fingers to her pulsing lips and spread her open to the cool night air. His thumb pressed upon a sensitive spot, and the glory of it made her moan.

"That's wonderful, my darling. I knew you'd be like this."

As he slid two fingers inside her, and when her drenched body greeted his possession, he paused to smile at her with a devil's victory.

She hailed his dominance as he caught her by the nape of her neck and held her to him as he stroked her once, twice, and ever so deeply once again. "I want only you, my sweet."

"Prove it," she begged for now, for always, for whatever that meant to him.

He bent to kneel upon the stone terrace and parted her skirts.

She wound her fingers into his thick silken curls and cravenly opened herself for him.

He groaned in approval, found her center, and kissed her as if he were tasting delicate offerings. At once, he parted her searing flesh wider and set his tongue to that same wild spot that had sent her careening into desperate abandon seconds ago.

"This is what I will give you every night," he whispered, his voice raw with animal hunger. He licked her with a rough torrid tongue that sent her wild.

She whimpered.

"I know, sweetheart. You are so giving," he said.

But he was the one who so generously gave her more ravishing kisses.

She needed everything of this bliss. "More," she cried.

"This then?" he asked, the heathen, as he nibbled at that same spot that drove her mad.

"Yes!" She dug her nails into his scalp.

And he licked her, his tongue persistent. He sucked her and kissed her until she stiffened and shattered into a kaleidoscope of colors. She sagged, and he caught her up in his arms as she floated down.

She raised her face to him, and he kissed her. The musky taste of her very self on his lips was an aphrodisiac she wanted yet again.

"Shall we have more of that forever, darling?" he asked her.

But an uproar came from the guests in the salon. People shouted, running toward the hall.

Heath turned as did she, alarmed.

"What's happening?" Caught in a hazy euphoria, she couldn't make sense of the noise. But she blinked and came to a frightening memory.

She'd attended a ball once in London where the chandelier fell upon the guests, and the burning candles had set several men and women aflame. Servants rushed for water. Guests rushed to disrobe, removing their shawls or their frock coats. Addy herself had torn at her petticoat and ripped off a good long strip to wrap a lady dressed in scarlet satin, whose glorious black hair was in flames. Anything was proper to end the torment of the afflicted. All were saved from serious injury. Even the woman Addy had helped had survived with good humor and a new haircut *a la Grecque*. The next day, the lady appeared at Cass's house in Mayfair with her thanks to Addy and sent bouquets of roses afterward for a week. As a delightful addition, the two had also become fast friends.

"We'll learn," Gyles said as he helped her right her skirts and cover her breasts. "But we will talk again afterward!"

The two of them hurried in the direction of the crowd toward the central stairs but stopped when they saw those who led a grand procession down.

Cass, a stern look upon her oval face, her pale blonde coiffure unnaturally mussed, descended arm-in-arm with Imogen on one side and Lex, the Earl of Martindale, on the other. Behind them came Cass's giant, stark and angry in his regimentals. Next to him strode their host and hostess, Lord and Lady Carlisle. All appeared as if they'd been cast in wax.

Laurel rushed forward in the crowd and reached Addy. "What's happened?"

"I've no idea, but Imogen has Cass's shawl about her and..."

Her bodice is torn!

She and Laurel ran to their sister's side. As ever, they always stood together in times of terror or loss.

Behind the Carstairs came two of their tall, liveried footmen, one to either side of a fuming Lord Wye. The man cursed, demanding the servants unhand him. But their master shook his head and said, "To the door with him."

Lord Carstairs watched the three march toward the foyer, then he spun. He stood at rigid attention and announced that the evening, sadly, was at an end. "We've had an unfortunate situation, but all is now resolved."

"Indeed." Beside him, Lady Carstairs smiled, but her expression was one of shattered glass. "We do have good news. Lady Downs, if you would, please?"

Cass smiled graciously at Martindale and took Imogen's hand to place in his. "This evening, my young cousin, Miss Imogen Devereaux, accepted the proposal of the Earl of Martindale to be his wife. We shall have the wedding at ten Friday morning. A breakfast to follow at our home in Charles Street. Many of you will attend, I do hope. We will be at home Thursday this week to receive afternoon calls and your congratulations."

Chapter Eight

T HE NEXT MORNING, breakfast talk for the women centered on preparations for Imogen's wedding. Addy tried to focus on it, but her scintillating interlude with Heath lived in her reverie like a golden dream. Risqué visions of him on his knees inspired hot shivers through her body. Remembered ecstasies of how she'd trembled under his tenderness turned her fierce and needy. No matter how much she wished to push him away for a few minutes at least, he lived, grinning and determined, in her reverie.

He had sealed himself to her and she to him. She could not do without him. Now or ever. She managed as best she could to participate and rejoice for her sister.

All three women managed to revive Imogen's spirits and propel her to realize that the best solution had come of the event. She'd wed a man she valued, and her groom had diffused a scandalous situation. Cass had described in great detail to Laurel and Addy last night how Imogen had been attacked by that scoundrel Lord Wye.

The triplets knew him well. He'd been so crass as to attempt to seduce Imogen back in Dublin long before Grandpapa passed away. Assaulting her in a garden maze, Wye had vowed to have her. Even wed her. Grandpapa had asked if Imogen agreed, and she'd told him the man was no one she'd ever want. When Wye pressed the matter and threatened Imogen with more scandal, she threatened him with an equal insult to the…well, to be honest…size of his manhood. Wye had withdrawn his offer. Now, they all knew he had retired harboring malice.

But Imogen's relationship with the Earl of Martindale, brief though it was, had blossomed and Lex had, in front of half of Brighton society, told everyone that Imogen had accepted his proposal of marriage. Whether all of that was as true as the description Cass gave to the two sisters, neither would dispute. Their middle sister was saved marriage to a bounder and a more severe scandal of Wye attacking her a second time. The Earl of Martindale had appeared at the house at nine o'clock this morning to talk with Cass, offer new solicitations to Imogen, and bid them all farewell as he left for London to acquire a marriage license.

Cass had immediately declared the day was meant for shopping for Imogen's trousseau. "It's just what you need. We will be seen, and we will be proud to be out among the *ton*."

Laurel and Imogen had hurried off to dress. Addy had begged off, using the excuse of weariness to buy time for herself alone. But Cass would not hear of it.

"Only if you arrive at Miss Maribel's Millinery Shop in Rose Lane promptly at eleven. And we leave you with Fifi."

Not precisely the maid Addy wished to accompany her. But the assignment made her wonder if Fifi had told Cass where they'd gone Sunday morning. And perhaps, even why.

The three women went off to shop as Addy lingered at the breakfast table.

The knocker of the front door clanged against the wood three times.

She rose and jumped when three more whacks of the knocker resounded up the stairs. Richards had cleared the sideboard long ago and was down in the kitchen.

The knocker banged. Harder this time.

Richards, poor man, was losing his hearing and, so far away, was not responding.

"I'm coming! I'm coming!" Addy sprang from her chair to

rush along the hall and down the stairs. When she opened the door, the man who stood there took her breath away.

"May I come in?" Gyles asked, hat in hand, his auburn hair gleaming in the morning sun, his beautiful eyes anxious.

She clutched her fichu to her throat. Hair up in a careless knot, she was in no state to converse with this man on her doorstep at ten in the morning. Yet the very sight of him set her blood racing, and her memory of last night made her hot and wet. She would never turn him away. "Please, do."

He rushed inside, where he took one long examination of the hall and stairs, then walked right up to her. Removing his hat, he threw it atop the hall table and ran a hand through his thick auburn hair. He had mint on his breath and a twinkle in his eye as he swept her into his arms. "Good morning."

Oh, it was, indeed, with him so dashing and oh, so eager for her. She quivered at his greeting. So quick and ardent, his manhood's urgent to claim her was a seduction in itself. She questioned if she'd ever find any other man so randy for her. So perfect for her sensuous nature.

But she had to be wise and not let her own desire for him outpace her common sense. "This is not proper. My family have gone to the Lanes to see dressmakers."

"I know. I saw them walking toward the Lanes as my carriage passed. I hoped I'd catch you. But alone, as well? Good timing and fate." He looked divine in a navy superfine frock coat, blue waistcoat, and smart cravat.

She was practically in *dishabille*. Wearing only two thin layers of muslin, her skin absorbed his body heat, and her nipples blossomed proud and aching against his firm chest. He pulled her more dearly close to him, and she sucked in her breath. Would that she could rub herself against him, he'd laugh and think her a cat. But he was too handsome, too elusive, and too unpredicta-ble—and she'd not pull away.

Ohh! She wanted to stomp on his foot. "Why are you here?"

He grinned wickedly. "To tell you what I'm doing, where I'm

going, so that you are kinder to me than you seem to be at the moment."

"I'm not...unkind."

"No, you're skeptical of what happened last night. I don't blame you. I did not do this courting of you in the right order. I'm here to correct that. For just as I would have gone on, there was that announcement of Imogen and Lex's, followed by that awful business of the footmen escorting Lord Wye out the door. You had to leave, and rightly so. But I had to come this morning to see you, kiss you, and explain."

That still did not fully tell her why he was here...or his reason for presuming he could embrace her so freely.

"I'm off to London, my darling."

"Oh." His news and his endearment hit her like a cricket bat. Where would he go? And leave her with this aching desire to have his hands all over her? The man was infuriating! "London. Why should I care to know this?"

"Because I am off to sort our future." His molten gaze fell over her lips that burned, her cheeks that flamed, and her nipples that were iron against the thin fabric covering her desire for him. "When I return, I'll give you more than last night."

She melted to a little puddle at the prospect and clutched handfuls of his frock coat. "More than kisses?"

He grabbed a fistful of her long hair and pulled her head back. His lips spoke on her own. "More ecstasy than you can count."

"A promise?"

"The biggest one I've ever made."

"And those moments will be just like that one?"

"No."

"No?" Her voice was a pathetic little squeak.

"They'll be better. And you and I will be in a big broad bed without any barriers to our endeavors."

Her imagination saw him, naked, tall, and lean, his muscles rippling, rigid and long against linen sheets. Her eyes widened and ran down his form.

"Yes," he whispered, "just like that."

She caught some sanity. "It's wicked of you to speak of such things so early in the morning."

He winked at her and put on his hat. "When you're wholly mine, any minute of the day will be divinely wicked."

That set fire to her longing for him.

"Be good until I return." Chuckling, he ran his fingers up into the wealth of her hair and held her there as he kissed her once again, this time like a Viking raider invading a round keep, taking a woman who should be his. "Then you and I will be naughty together."

He opened the door and turned to look over his shoulder.

"How can you leave me…?" *Wanting you?*

He hooted. "I see you'd prefer I stay. But dangerous, that, my sweet. You'll recover. I want to see you bloom for me when I return."

"Oh, go! You terrible man. Making me guess what in the world you are about!" *Being too damn cryptic.*

"I save my best words for the finest ending. Awful of me, but do remember, darling. I love you." He widened his eyes as he affirmed that with one nod. Then he put on his hat and left her standing alone at the door wishing she could take him to bed.

She shook there for many more minutes watching him leave. Blinking away the confusion of what had just happened, she frowned, shook her head, and finally, trudged up the stairs.

Men, she concluded, needed women to bring them to their senses. But of course, at the moment, she had none of her own.

Minutes later, she realized she rather liked that. She was indeed senseless from Gyles's kisses—and because she loved him, that made perfect sense.

The threat of ruin because Grandpapa had been less than an honest man drifted away in a new euphoria.

TWO DAYS LATER, Gyles settled into the squabs of his coach. He would miss his friend Lex's wedding to Imogen tomorrow, but he had laid out his reasoning and apologized for his inability to appear. Lex, a gracious fellow, had understood.

Speed was what Gyles was after to settle his own affairs. Now that the house on the Steine was fully staffed, aired, and appointed, he had dealt with his parents this morning. They were angry he'd left the pavilion but saw there was nothing they could do about it. They would face more that they could not change in a few days.

He sighed. The driver pulled away with all due speed for the north road to London. Eager was too mild a word to describe Gyles's intentions to speak with his new solicitor.

He had engaged the new man last year for himself alone. Quietly. The group whom his father and his grandfather before him had employed for decades had served ably. Indeed, the family solicitors for the Dukes of Stonegage had a long history of loyalty, as they should. However, upon Gyles's return to London once Napoleon was in Elba, he had received so many appeals by his father to hand over hundreds of pounds to pay debtors that Gyles had sought a way to ensure the duke learned nothing of his own finances. On advice of the new solicitor, Gyles had switched banks, and the new bankers were duty-bound to reveal nothing of his affairs to anyone, even his father.

But he had need of that same solicitor now to build a stronger wall between the Stonegage influence and his own. Gyles would not be thwarted in the matter of choosing a bride by his father's petty desire for a painting. The duke might want it as a matter of family pride, or he could covet it in the hope of selling it to line his coffers. Family pride had not influenced his father to try to borrow funds to ransom Gyles away from the French thirteen years ago.

Bankruptcy had been his father's excuse then. Gyles had never questioned the viability of that. The matter of Gyles's marriage was not, at heart, a money matter. Not for Gyles, who was flush and could marry the poorest girl on earth if he so chose. For his father, however, finances had always been a touchy subject. Now he would not permit the duke to dictate his future happiness by denying him the woman he wanted as wife. By the grace of God, Gyles had survived his father's inability to pay his ransom.

Indeed, he'd survive his father's latest challenge, full bore.

"To deny your father the ability to approve your marriage courts disaster, Heath." His good friend Hadley Sherborne, Viscount Grey, had been most adamant in his warning about it the other morning as he and Fitz accompanied him on his search for a rental house. Gyles had heard of Grey's arrival last Friday in Brighton from Martindale. Learning of Grey's particular troubles with his own father over an offer of marriage to a woman his father did not approve of, Gyles called upon him at Grey's summer home on the Steine. He needed perspective on how to fight his own father's opposition to his pursuit of Addy.

"I expect a war," Gyles said and waved away the Grey butler's offer of coffee or breakfast. Grey looked the worse for his worries over how to win back the woman he truly loved. His golden hair was askew, and his forest green eyes were red with lack of sleep. Rumor had it Grey was in town to woo Laurel Devereaux back to his arms. "But it's thirty-three years late for my father to disown me. My parents' signatures on the day of their wedding are in the chapel registry at home. The name of my mother nor my date of birth cannot—woe unto my father—be denied."

"Ha!" His friend chuckled as he used his serviette to wipe the corners of his mouth. "Mine threatened it anyway."

Gyles scoffed. "How?"

"Follow Shakespeare's advice. 'First we kill all the lawyers.'"

"My father might think of that. Though I will say," Gyles sighed, "that he is not one to give over to me easily."

"Superiority is drilled into them from birth."

Gyles countered with a grin. Indeed, his friend's father was a noted peer of the realm valued for his blue blood—and his arcane stubbornness. "A trait they've engendered in us, too."

"Imprisonment had as much to do with yours." His friend knew well his past.

"Ever since the little French Emperor sought to lock me away at the ripe young age of twenty, I've nurtured a singular irreverence for hare-brained authority." Gyles would not share the shame of his father's failure to ransom him from the French.

"I've not had the distinct displeasure of Bony's shackles, but I have experienced the demands of my own sire. Trust me, they are as infuriating if not as debilitating."

Gyles trod carefully on his friend's sensibilities. "Am I right that you yourself are here in town to correct the disaster your father made of your proposal to a certain lady?"

Grey considered the depths of his coffee cup. "I gather the *ton* has the word on it?"

"What say you, my friend?" Gyles would not ask which lady Grey sought. He knew the two-year-old story of Grey's enchantment with an Irish girl. His friend had sought to marry her until his father had called him home to Amesbury and demanded he betroth himself to the young woman whose land marched along their own in Wiltshire.

"Last week, my aunt wrote to my mother," he told Gyles. "She said that the three granddaughters of the Earl of Barry had arrived for the Season. My mother let it slip, and I had to come. I have to try to make amends to Laurel."

Gyles pitied the man. "I wish you *bonne chance*, my friend. Can I help you in any way?"

"Good of you, Heath. But first, you must find a genie who can cast a spell to let me darken the door of number twenty Charles Street."

"Surely, the lady can forgive you."

"Can she?" Grey scoffed. "Perhaps if I come bearing myself on a platter."

He'd thought Laurel Devereaux serene, even retiring. "She's bloodthirsty, eh?"

"A dragon! When last we met, she breathed fire. 'Come near me, and I'll have your twiddle-dees for breakfast.'"

Gyles winced, expressed his sorrow, and soon left his beleaguered friend.

As Gyles settled back into his coach for the long ride to London, he vowed to solve his problems quickly and hurry back to Brighton. Regardless of his solicitor's findings, Heath swore to collect the bride he desired above all others.

Chapter Nine

Laurel pulled Addy aside as they made their way down the stairs to receive guests for their last regular salon the day before Imogen's wedding. "I've terrible news."

"Oh, no." Addy halted, one hand to the banister. She hoped that word of Imogen's wedding would erase any rumors about the devilish attack by Wye and even any tidbits about the nefarious doings of Grandpapa. "What is it?"

"I had a note just now from my friend, Lady Susanna Fortescue. She's staying with her parents over at the Old Ship Hotel. You will never guess who appeared for dinner last night at the Prince Regent's?"

"Tell me." If it was Wye, Cass would send a note over to Imogen's fiancé, Martindale, who would frog march the fellow from Brighton in a minute. If the surprise visitor were someone from Dublin with intimate knowledge of Grandpapa or his activities, she would tell Cass that, too. Their cousin always had a means to put good words into the social stream. She gripped Laurel's wrist. "Who is it?"

"Lord Grey."

The viscount was the very man Laurel wished would die a thousand deaths. "He's here with his new wife?"

"No. Unmarried."

"How can that be?" Grey had met and courted Laurel when they were all in Dublin before Grandfather took ill and retired to his bed. Addy was confused. The man was to have married some girl his father decreed acceptable. "Wasn't June to be the wedding? What happened? Did he jilt her, too?"

That seemed logical since that was precisely what he'd done when he offered marriage to Laurel and withdrew when his papa demanded he propose to another lady.

Laurel snorted. "Why not? He knows how to do that and avoid the *ton*'s censure."

Addy stared at Laurel, suspicious of the evil glint in her sister's eye. "Why do you care that he's here? You sent him packing when he came carrying the ashes of his promise. So why?"

"He is a good friend of your Heath."

The relevance of that escaped Addy. "And so?"

"Did you invite Heath to the wedding tomorrow?"

"No. He cannot attend." Addy rushed on, avoiding a discussion of what she knew of Gyles's journey to London and his promises to return to court her. "And in any case, Cass has carefully chosen the guest list to a few good friends of hers. That way, word goes out that the bride was lovely and dewy-eyed, the groom besotted, and the wedding breakfast a joyful occasion. Whatever that villain Lord Wye put out about the event or its cause will be drowned in the details."

"Grey would not dare to come on his own. Do you think?"

Addy heard her sister's fear and took her sister's hand. "He's not welcome. He knows that. Any fool who had done what he did would stay far away."

Laurel frowned.

Addy gave her a consoling smile. Calling Grey a fool was going too far. Laurel, for all her turmoil over the man's desertion, could label him all sorts of names, but others best tread lightly.

"Come, let's go down," Addy encouraged her. "We'll brighten Imogen's smile. She's accomplished her goal here in Brighton, and we must show her our support."

"You're right. This is the beginning of Imogen's new life. I will miss her, but I am happy for her."

Addy had rejoiced that Imogen had found such a good man to marry. The catastrophe of Imogen's ruin had been averted by the quick response of the Earl of Martindale. He had done a favor to Addy and Laurel by his proposal. Saving the entire family's reputation was reason alone for a woman to love a man.

Would that Laurel could live down the damage done to her by Lord Grey jilting her. And that she would remain unblemished, not only for her own self-respect but also for the man she chose as her own.

Addy's hopes winged to Gyles, that he, above all others she had met, could value her enough to return and fulfill his promises of a proposal and marriage.

A FEW GUESTS had already arrived, and they set the salon atwitter with congratulations for the bride and her family. Addy loved the gaiety of the moment and how it washed away all the bitterness of the scenes that had precipitated it.

Lord Hewitt came and made a nuisance of himself by enjoying too much wine and gushing over each sister. Lord Penhurst and the Duke of Lonsdale arrived one after the other, which made Addy wonder if they timed their appearances closely. Colonel Lord Welles soon appeared and greeted Cass with a Continental kiss on the hand. He was certainly a striking figure, now in superbly cut street clothes and carving quite a swath through the feminine crowd. Cass could not take her eyes from him, even as the man carefully and pointedly made his preference well known as he stood with Cass and never left her side.

Among them, the latest to arrive was the curate, John Fellowes.

Nearest the entry to the salon, it fell to Addy to engage him. "We're delighted to see you here today, sir. So many have come to wish Imogen well."

He gave her a tight smile as if it pained him to lift the corners of his mouth. "I have come strictly to enjoy your company, Miss Adelaide."

"That is most complimentary, sir. I'm glad you are enjoying yourself in Brighton."

"My father," he said with emphasis, "I'm sure you've heard of the Earl of Davenport. He was most insistent that I come and meet you and your two sisters."

"That's very thoughtful of him." She had no idea who his father was, but evidently, the man was attuned to gossip of the comings and goings of people in Brighton. She also heard in Fellowes's tone his aspiration to be her suitor. With his position as curate, she knew enough of the status of English peerage to understand that as a younger son, he had to make his own way.

A spot in the Church's hierarchy was the most glory a curate could claim, as the pay for such a lowly spot was nigh unto nothing. His father, the earl, must have some knowledge of her dowry of two thousand. But that would not buy enough food for even two seasons. So Mister Fellowes, poor man, was hoping for a miracle that she might favor him with her hand.

"You don't know my father, do you?" He bent close, shrewd wickedness bright in his eyes.

"No." Addy had a moment of discontent. Was the Curate Fellowes purposely impressing her or intimidating her? "I must confess, I do not keep up on everyone's status as I should. But do tell me about yourself, sir. You have an assignment in a local parish, as I understand it?"

Smiling as if he had a mouthful of sugar, he puffed himself up with his pride of place. "I do. I have recently taken a position as curate in a small parish in West Sussex. Not far from here. It provides me a good living."

Addy nodded. What was "good" for one was starvation for another.

"I have a cottage," he was quick to add. "My own allotment."

"A-allotment?"

"A plot where I grow my own vegetables."

"I see." Lost as to what she was to think of this, she grasped at an idea. "Are you a good gardener, then?"

"I learn."

"Oh." She had repeatedly tried to "learn" how to grow squash and lettuces and had managed to support the growth of beetles more than plants. "I'm better at gathering herbs and medicinals from the forest."

"What?" He blinked, not only shocked but worried. "You mix potions?"

"Potions. No. I make herbal remedies that help those who suffer—"

"You must stop."

"I must?" She was astonished at his effrontery to suggest such a thing.

"For your immortal soul. You must not engage in devil's work."

"But it isn't that at all."

"You try to cure people of maladies?"

"I do."

"A trained chemist is the man to do such a thing."

"That's not necessarily true." According to Drusinda, chemists erred. Mister Algood was trained but didn't know everything. "Women are capable, too."

"No, no. Never." He snatched her hand and held her in such a grip that she flinched but could not move. "You must repent the error of your ways. All of them. So many, too."

"What?"

"I understand you kiss men. Many men." He sought her answer, but alarm rang in her head that he wanted to chastise her for it.

"Well, I—"

"This is unacceptable."

As are you, sir.

"You must cease and desist."

"I have not kissed—"

"Repent!" He lifted a forefinger to the heavens. "Repent the error of your ways!"

"I do try—"

"Your two sisters need strong men to temper their Irish shenanigans."

She yanked her hand from his. "I beg your pardon, sir."

"No wonder a creature like that Wye has no compunctions about attacking your sister."

"Excuse me, sir." She snatched up her skirts, her cheeks burning and her heart pulsing with indignation. "I must see to our other guests."

"I wish to help you." He snatched at her hand. "I can save you. Marry me, and you shall have redemption."

Over my dead body.

"I can help you achieve the purity of soul you need to reach the pearly gates."

She glared at him. *What an arrogant ass.*

"And some people think *I* am self-indulgent!" She fumed as she marched away.

She headed straight for the retiring room to collect her ravaged mind, one conclusion firmly fixed there. She would rather live in the woods like a hermit than marry a man of the cloth. Indeed, if he tried to save her from her 'shenanigans,' she'd happily bury Fellowes in his allotment.

FRIDAY MORNING, GYLES alighted from his coach at the red brick building of his solicitors' offices in the City. The plain white wooden sign, "Timmons and Hastings," banged to and fro in the breeze. He entered the modest reception room to find the same thin, eagle-nosed clerk who'd been there when first Gyles came last year, sitting at the desk.

The man scrambled to his feet. "My lord."

Gyles removed his hat and gloves. "Good afternoon. Mister Simpson, I believe your name is?"

"I am, sir. How do you do?"

"I am very well, thank you. I'm here to see Mr. Willard Timmons."

"Certainly, sir. We received your letter of instructions. I shall alert Mister Timmons for you. May I bring you a tea or brandy?"

"No, sir. Thank you very much. I'm quite fine as I am."

Simpson ushered him straight into his employer and closed the door behind him.

"Hello, Willard. How are you?"

"Very good to see you, sir." Timmons was a youthful-looking man, perhaps forty, with a smile and handshake as strong as an ox. He offered the chair before his broad desk. "Please have a seat. I'm delighted you've come."

"I am thrilled that you can see me so readily. I hope you have been able to look at my situation."

"I have, sir. In fact, it has not taken me long to research most of the particulars of your case. I can give you a few answers."

"Wonderful. I'm eager to resolve any challenge with my father's requests."

"We'll start from what I have found. Your father continues on a regular basis each year to enclose his lands at the rate of one hundred acres up to nearly one thousand acres. The Enclosure Law of roughly thirty years ago allows him to do this. I have surveyed the numbers of tenants as best I can, and more than forty-odd have left in the past two years. From what I can tell, that land they tilled lies fallow."

"Unproductive," Gyles said with a sigh. There was another cause of his father's failed income and his need for Gyles to support him.

"Many of those tenants who remain are angry at him, not only because their friends and family have gone, but also because the duke has given orders over the years to set fire to cottages of those who left." Willard winced. "His Grace told them this assures those who go may not return."

"And most likely never wish to."

Willard nodded, looked at his notes, and settled back in his chair. "With crop failures on the rest of the duchy's lands and no investment in hoes or plows or animals, the estate yields drop even more precipitously."

Gyles wrestled with his anger at his father. It would be so easy to rant and rave, but he'd learned that doing so only brought him to the edge of one of his blinding attacks.

"You may continue to do as you wish in regard to administering your own land, my lord. Your father has never expressed interest in trying to control it. What you give to your father in terms of money—whether as gift or loan—is also at your discretion."

"Can he refuse to sign any papers recognizing a wife of mine as my marchioness or later her becoming my duchess?"

"We cannot find such legal details on such short notice, my lord. Much of that is in your father's solicitors' keeping. I am sorry."

Gyles rapped his fingers on the chair rest. Because Gyles's title and lands came to the family via a second cousin of the Whitmore family more than a century ago, Gyles administered his own lands. But Gyles worried more that, to the terms of the dower and the coverture, his father might still be an impediment. "He can still object to the marriage."

"Sadly, yes. He can refuse to sign."

"We will have to make it impossible then for him to refuse."

"You have means, my lord."

"I do. We'll use the power of my purse, Willard. That which matters most to him. We will start by telling him he may have loans from me semi-annually only if he follows my orders. I will stipulate that he cannot continue to sell unentailed land. He must stop all enclosure of other acreage. Finally, he may not destroy any cottages of any tenants, in use or vacated. Finally, there will be no more loans *ever* unless he signs the marriage agreement.

Not a penny."

At ten o'clock on Friday morning, Imogen wed the Earl of Martindale and became his countess. She wore one of her new gowns, a flowing aquamarine satin with a white corsage of shantung shot with silver. She sparkled in the morning light as she spoke her vows to the man who could not take his eyes from hers.

Addy sipped champagne and watched the groom hover so near his bride. He cared for her more than they knew. She could hope for the same beguiled look upon her own groom's face the day they married and ever after.

"A charming couple," said the curate John Fellowes as he stepped near.

Addy bristled. She'd been aware the man was among those on Cass's carefully chosen guest list. When she asked why he was to attend, Cass had told her his father and mother were influential in society. One had to invite him to remain in the Earl of Davenport's good graces.

"They are indeed," she said and sought an opening among the other guests' conversations so that she could escape.

He caught the chill of her words, wincing. "I was pleased to be invited here today."

To that, she merely stared into his watery blue eyes.

"I gather you had nothing to do with that, Miss Adelaide."

She caught the worried frown of Cass from across the room. "You owe the invitation to my cousin, Lady Downs. And if you will excuse me, sir, I must welcome—"

He blocked her path. "Welcome me, Miss Adelaide."

She turned a critical eye on him.

He grabbed her hand. "I wish to apologize."

She tugged her fingers from his angry hold. "Good of you.

Now if—"

"Please don't leave me. I regret my outburst of the other day."

"As you should, sir."

"I merely wished to save you from yourself."

She scoffed. "Sir, save yourself first."

"I—I don't understand."

"Repent of your pride to think you can direct me to follow your orders."

He pulled his little chin back into his neck. "I do not know what you mean."

"Exactly." She sighed. "Perspective on one's own behavior is vital to a well-lived life."

His eyes turned sharp and narrow. "You correct me?"

"You need it," she said with a certain measure of glee and left him where he stood.

Chapter Ten

MISSING IMOGEN WAS a bigger hurdle than Addy expected. The three Barry girls, once known in Waterford and Dublin as a trio of scamps who raced through town on spirited horses or danced long into the night at any ball, had taken Brighton by storm. Imogen, in a few days, had met her earl and married him. Leaving Addy and Laurel to conquer the other gentlemen who came to Brighton to see and be seen and court.

The parties they attended that Saturday and Sunday were filled with those who wished to learn more about the newlyweds or Addy and Laurel's own intentions with any gentlemen with whom they danced or talked. Looking for the current gossip, many like Lady Forbish asked leading questions about Imogen's feelings for the earl, her new husband.

"Love him, does she?" the woman asked Addy that Sunday evening at a ball given by a baron of some renown and wealth.

"Yes, of course, she does, my lady." *What gall to ask such a thing.*

"He did the right thing to save her."

To which Addy did not bat an eyelash.

"But of course, the man is the picture of health. Much like his friend, the Marquess of Heath."

Was the woman fishing for intimate knowledge of Addy's regard for Gyles?

The lady snapped open her fan and regarded with bored eyes

those dancing a country set. "You know Heath, do you not?"

"I do, ma'am." *How had she gotten stuck talking to this annoying woman? Where was Cass? Or Laurel?*

"Word is that he regards you highly."

A gush of warm desire for Gyles flew through Addy's veins. "That is a fine compliment."

"More than, my girl." Forbish snapped her fan shut and poked the point of her sticks into Addy's breast bone. "He seeks to engage himself to you."

Addy swallowed. "The *ton* says this?"

"Despite his father's opposition."

Addy could not deny it. "Most regrettable."

"What will you do about it?"

"I?"

The woman curved up her thin lips into a saccharine smile. "You."

Addy lifted her shoulders. "I have not met his father and have no inkling of the source of his disapproval."

The woman laughed, a shrill note of derision. "Your grandfather had quite a reputation."

Anger at the impending insult colored her vision red. "He is dead now, my lady. Whatever he did is past."

"But his treasures survive. I understand the Barry solicitors in Dublin sell what they can."

Should she even be listening to this? "Lady Forbish, whoever is your source is either close to the solicitors in Dublin or fabricates the whole story."

"But they do exist? Your grandfather's so-called treasures?"

Addy looked her squarely in the eyes. She did not know much about the law, but she would not be sucked into admitting knowledge of any crime to such a harpy. She'd spread it about Brighton before breakfast. "Since you know so much, Lady Forbish, why not write to the solicitor in Dublin yourself? Ask him anything you wish to know, but my family and I have nothing to say to you. And now, do understand, I find I must seek more pleasant company."

Addy marched away, the look on her face startling a few whom she passed. *The nerve, the gall!*

Imagine asking someone if one of their beloved family were a thief! Why, she ought to march right over to the town gossip, Countess of Huntington, and tell her a thing or two. Except, bah! What good would that do? She had nothing juicy to tell the town crier.

Heading straight for the terrace, Addy blindly wound her way down the garden path. She needed solitude. Fresh air. A summer breeze in her hair. The kiss of stars upon her brow. A soothing fragrance of roses and lavender.

"I say, Miss Adelaide."

No. No, no. Not Fellowes. Again.

She whirled toward the voice.

"What do you want, sir? I am in no mood to deal with you or your ultimatums."

"I'm here to help you."

Do what? Help? Ha! She gripped her indignation in a stranglehold and sighed. "Thank you, sir. I wish to be alone."

"But I offer you a friend."

You? Hmm. The price for that would be high. "A friend."

In the moonlight, he appeared softer, more a gentleman than he had heretofore proven to be. "You wish to be my friend?"

At that, he beamed. His little crooked teeth shone bright white in his happy smile. "I earnestly do."

"Prove it."

"In any way, Miss Adelaide," he said as he gallantly offered her a bow. "I am your servant."

"What gossip is there about my family?"

He snapped backward at that. "Oh, I doubt that—"

"Come now. You implied it. Others do, too. Tell me what is rumored about myself and my sisters. My Grandpapa, too."

Fellowes cleared his throat. "You and your sisters were terrors in Dublin."

"How?"

"Well, um…as children. You stole items from stores." *That had been Imogen.* "And you could copy someone's handwriting to get them to hand over their family jewels." *Laurel had done that once, and Grandpapa had made her return the rubies to Lady Dunmare.*

"And me?"

He waved a dismissive hand. "I told you that the other day. I won't repeat it."

Why not admit it? "That I kiss a lot of men."

He flinched. "You do."

She inhaled and considered the mellow light of the moon. "And my grandfather? What word of him?"

"Your grandfather, it is said, was a master at valuing art. Paintings, mostly. Some sculpture. A few other items, such as jewelry."

"I see." She trod closer to the fellow who could chastise her without a qualm but who recited her grandfather's expertise. Meanwhile, he sweated like a pig. "For example, what did Grandpapa do?"

"The late Earl of Barry made his income by taking in stolen art and selling it privately. He took only items he could authenticate himself as the work of a master."

"And who were his clientele?" she asked.

"Ah. Those who bought?"

"Precisely, sir."

"Everyone who had the blunt."

"And so, the gossips spread this about us three sisters for the fun of it."

He pressed his skinny little lips together.

"But they speak of Grandpapa's work and hope they can get their rightful possessions back."

"Yes."

"But they cannot unless they pay a current value for the art. Am I right?"

"True," he said. "And many cannot afford to buy theirs back."

"Many of the works are that valuable?"

"They are," he said. "Napoleon stole so much from so many countries for more than twenty years. He carted it all to Paris for his Louvre that the palaces of Europe are bare! If anyone has anything left of any value these days, it's a miracle. Your Grandfather is one such person."

"I see," she said with reluctance. "For example? What works is he reputed to have in his collection?"

"A portrait of Francis the First of France by Leonardo Da Vinci. A few Greek statues. One by an Italian artist."

A DaVinci she could acknowledge was a rare find. Old statues, well, someone must like them. She wondered if Gyles's parents had dealt with Grandpapa. "Any idea what the Duke of Stonegage wants of Grandpapa's collection?"

"A portrait of the first Countess of Heath by Hans Holbein."

Addy knew little of art, but of Holbein she had heard. That alone told her the item in question had to be worth thousands. As for the rest, whatever the artist or previous owner, what good did the treasures do where they are? Rotting, unseen, and unloved.

"Thank you, Fellowes." She swung toward the terrace doors, eager to go home. "I appreciate your help."

He stepped toward her, eager as a rabbit. "Might I accompany you, Miss Adelaide?"

Some men never learned to fade away, did they? "Thank you, Fellowes, no."

→»»×«««

MONDAY MORNING, SHE received a letter from Gyles. He planned to arrive in Brighton today, his challenges, he said, "solved." Her heart pounding in expectation, she was fairly bursting with joy. But she would not enflame Laurel nor Cass's hopes until he appeared and asked for her hand.

Throwing herself into her lessons with Drusinda, she had

gone to visit the fortune-tellers while Cass and Laurel had attended church yesterday. Today, she planned the same.

"You must come with us, Addy," Laurel beseeched her. "You always love new ribbons."

"I do. But I have no need for more." She threw a smile toward Cass. "You've been so generous with us. I will not overburden you."

"I would heckle you to come with us, but I think I see a new facet to your character, my dear."

"I thank you for the compliment."

Cass covered her hand and squeezed it. "Fifi has told me you go to the foreigners for instruction. I don't approve the teachers, but I do approve you learning the finer art."

"I'm glad you do!" Addy beamed at her.

"If we each knew more how to cure people of their maladies, we would all be happier. More productive, too. Do go. And ask Mister Algood to give you another prescription for my monthly aches, will you?"

Many women suffered pain and discomfort with their monthly flows. "I did not know you had such a problem. I'll ask him."

"Good. Thank you. Take Fifi with you."

Addy rolled her eyes at that.

"I know, I know!" said Cass and stifled a laugh. "She hates to go to that part of town, but do take her."

Two hours later, Addy led the way toward the Lanes with Fifi grumbling in French as she trudged behind.

"Why not stop here, Fifi?" Addy tipped her parasol toward the sweet shop and dug in her reticule for a few guineas. "Do go inside. It might rain. Have an ice or a bun, and I will return in minutes. No need to come along."

The French maid gave her a frown but valiantly surrendered with a shrug.

Addy hurried away.

Traffic in the part of the Lanes where Drusinda had her shop was thin this time of day. Those who sought spells or fortunes came more often at night. Yet Addy thought she heard footsteps marching in time with hers along the cobbles. When she slowed, they did. When she stopped, so did they.

She shook off the feeling and hastened on her way.

Yet at the corner of the road that led down to Drusinda's, she heard some running toward her. And she spun.

"What are you doing?" She couldn't believe it. "Why are you here? With that...?"

A cloth was pressed to her nose.

She writhed and yelled, but her cry came out muffled to her ears. "Wha ish the meanung of—"

That was a stupid question. She knew the meaning.

Bugger! She whacked him about the head with her parasol. Then elbowed him in the ribs.

He grunted and groaned.

She kicked back to strike his legs.

He cursed.

But in the end, he was more powerful than she. And so was the potion he had sprinkled in his cloth. She felt her strength die, coughing at his acidic concoction and sinking into his arms like a withering flower.

Chapter Eleven

CASS TOOK FIFI by the shoulders. "What do you mean she disappeared?"

"She is gone. *Pouf! Pouf!*" The maid was rabid. Her hair down, her skirts askew from running all the way home. "Like...like Fouché would take a woman—she'd be no more!"

Cass scowled at her. "Fouché does not have power here. Who took her? When? How?"

"I do not know, *Madame*. The *gitan* says *Mademoiselle* never came. *Pouf! She is gone!*"

Cass ran a hand through her hair. "The fortune-teller did not see anyone abduct her?"

"Only a little man. No chin! Big nose, *Madame*."

"No chin? Big nose?" Cass frowned.

Laurel slapped a hand to her cheek. "The curate! What's his name?"

Fifi shook her head.

Cass stared at Laurel. "Fellowes?"

"The Earl of Davenport's boy? He hasn't half a brain to play with!" She snapped her fingers and ran to pull the bell.

Within a minute, Richards bustled in. "My lady?"

"Run to St. James's Street, number two, and tell Colonel Lord Welles I need him immediately. Addy's gone. It's a matter of life and death."

"WHO IS THIS you suspect?" Welles gripped Cass's hands. Her maddeningly marvelous lover was well turned out in black and fawn superfine street clothes, a hulking and comforting presence in the small room.

Laurel, Richards, and Fifi stood agape in fear.

"He's Davenport's boy, Magnus." Cass fought tears, and Magnus thumbed them away from her cheeks. "The earl's fourth son. A little fellow. Simpers, actually."

"Fellowes." Laurel wrung her hands, a frantic look to her large jade eyes. "No chin. Big nose."

"Addy complained to me about him pestering her," Cass said. "He's a pimple on the arse of society. Or...well, that's what Addy said of him. There is no one else of whom she complained so bitterly."

Laurel snorted. "He wants to save her from herself. Thinks she needs to be more conservative. Should be a nice little mouse. Not kiss men."

"What? But she hasn't!" Cass was now furious. "She re-formed. Promised me when we came here. And she did. She did! What is he talking about?"

"And now she's gone!" Laurel stepped toward Cass.

"Shhh, quiet now, both of you." Welles gathered both Cass and Laurel into his bear-like embrace. "Listen to me. Tell me where he lives."

Cass thought a moment. "With his father, the Earl of Davenport. In a townhouse in Hove. West of here. Fellowes stays there with the earl for a few weeks on holiday."

"Wants a wife," said Laurel. "Adelaide, to be precise."

"But she doesn't want him," Cass said. "All the more reason for him to take her."

"She insulted him," Laurel said.

Cass turned to her. "What do you mean?"

"She did! Well, he insulted her first. So she had to give him the cut, didn't she?'"

"The earl? Tell me about him." Welles lifted Cass's chin. "Is he one of these righteous types? Must I go in all hellfire and brimstone?"

Cass shook her head. "I don't know him that well."

"I'll use it on him anyway. Works best when cooperation is the goal. I'll need one or two more men. And Heath's best friend is Martindale, but he's in London on his honeymoon with Adelaide's sister," Welles said with a quick glance toward Laurel. "I wish to take a few friends. For one, Heath's and my mutual one."

Cass noted he let the question of the identity of his friend hang in the air for Laurel's consideration.

Laurel looked miserable. "Anyone who can get Addy back, I applaud. Of course. Ask Lord Grey."

"We need him, sweetheart."

"I know, Cass. We cannot call up the watch. The scandal would be so great we'd never live it down."

Cass sniffed. "Exactly. And we must get Addy back without her being ruined."

"What of Fellowes?" Laurel said, anger mixed with her tears. "*He* needs to be ruined! A man of the cloth abducting a woman. It's outrageous."

Cass hugged her close, but her gaze was on Welles. "Get Grey. He'll have servants he trusts. The Grey Mansion on the Steine is his family's, and they are known for hiring footmen who are strapping big men."

"Consider it done!"

THE SUN SHONE over Brighton in a lovely blaze of summer light as Gyles's traveling coach pulled up to his new rental on the Steine. Across the street, a few houses north, he noticed odd activity at Grey's family home.

He alighted and took another look. Three fine horses were

reined to the post. But what made him startle were the rifles strapped to all the saddles.

"Go home, Shelby," he told his groom. "Alert the other grooms in the mews that I need my stallion. At once. Oh, and James," he said to his valet whom he'd brought down from London with him, "prepare the master suites as best you can."

Curious, he crossed the busy thoroughfare and walked into the wide-open front door. Going up the main stairs was Grey's butler, normally as placid as still water. At the sound of Gyles's footsteps, the old man whirled and stared at him, shaking. "What's the matter, Porter?"

"Terrible, my lord. A lady is missing."

"Awful news. Who is it?"

Porter winced, the old man not able to keep concern from his rheumy eyes, "One of those pretty Irish girls."

Gyles went still as death. "Which?"

"Miss Adelaide Devereaux. Abducted."

His heart dropped to the floor. "Grey knows?"

"Aye, sir. He's in the family library. Upstairs."

Passing around Porter, Gyles took the stairs two at a time and entered the room like the furies were after him. Three men stood there. Grey checked his pistol. A giant of a man sheathed his sword. Fitz examined his dagger.

"Grey!" He waited not for formalities. "Porter tells me that Adelaide has been abducted?"

"It's true. She did not return home from the Lanes an hour or so ago."

Heath could barely form the words. "Do we know who did this?"

The giant in town clothes struck first with a nod of his head. "Colonel Magnus Welles, sir. Cass and her cousin Laurel suspect it was a curate by the name of John Fellowes. He's a simpleton, lives in Hove with his papa."

"Not for long, he doesn't." Wild with fear and anger, Heath took stock of the men before him. All fit young men. Just what he needed to get his darling back.

Chapter Twelve

RACING AT TOP speed along the Marine Parade, the four horsemen reined in before the red brick mansion of the Earl of Davenport as the sun was setting.

"I'll go first," Gyles told Grey, Captain Fitzroy, and Colonel Lord Magnus Augustus Welles.

Gyles bounded up the steps and banged on the front door. When the butler gingerly opened it, Gyles pushed it wide. "The son. John. Where is he?"

The butler, a formidable stuffy type, sought to puff himself up and bar the entrance. Gyles would have none of it. "Your master? Tell him the Marquess of Heath is here with Lord Grey, Colonel Lord Welles, and Captain Fitzroy. We demand to know the whereabouts of John Fellowes."

When the butler tut-tutted him, Gyles grabbed him by the collar of his elaborately folded stock and said, "Now is the time, man."

"Y-yes. Yes, sir." And off he scurried up the main stairs.

"What is this? What intrusion is this?" came the insulted cry of an older man as he bustled along and finally stepped into view at the landing above.

"Your son, sir!" Gyles demanded of him. "Where is he?"

"You have no right—"

"I have every right. He has abducted my fiancée, sir. Is he here? If so, *where?*"

"He has done no such thing!"

Gyles had a moment when despair and brilliant flashing shards of a coming headache shot through him. He bit his lower lip. *Not now, dammit!*

'*Breathe, my darling,*' he heard Addy urge him. Indeed, the past few days, when all hell was amiss with negotiating his mistress's pension, he had found calm in the midst of the storm. He'd used Addy's syrup. He'd even refused all wine and whisky. He had improved. But this stress...

He slapped one hand to the huge silver carved newel...and quieted his nerves. He removed his pistol from its holster inside his frock coat and slowly looked up.

A wisp of a man appeared beside the earl. The two of them looked like peas in a pod. Wimps.

"How dare you come into my father's home!"

His weapon pointed, Gyles was halfway up the stairs and climbing.

Little pea was stepping backward, or rather scurrying back like a rat.

"Where is she?" Gyles demanded, and gaining him, lifted him with one hand by his pompously tied stock.

Fellowes choked. "I—I can't—"

"Where!?" Gyles shook him, and his little crooked teeth rattled.

"I—I just wanted to talk to her."

"Where?" he boomed.

"John!" His father a-fixed his monocle to his left eye. "You told me you'd—"

"Abducted her!" Gyles yelled. "That's what he did. Where is she?"

"I—I put her in the stables."

"Stables!" Gyles pushed him toward the stairs. "You little turd! Lead on!"

"John!" His father, breathing hard, grew florid and apoplectic. "You said—you said you'd put her in—"

"Yes, well, doesn't matter where, *does it, 'Dad'?*" Gyles sneered and pushed the boy down more steps. "He's got her, and you allowed it!"

Fellowes was suffering a bit of a rough patch getting down quickly enough for him. At the bottom, he stood, weaving in place as Gyles grabbed a fistful of his coat and bellowed, "Out now! The stables, man. Step to it!"

Gyles trooped Fellowes through the house to the back stairs, his three companions following. A stammering, stupefied earl brought up the rear. At the kitchen door, four servants stood agog as the parade passed them by into the small kitchen garden. Before them loomed the stables. The double wooden door stood open, and Gyles pushed Fellowes through.

"Adelaide!" Gyles yelled.

But when no sound issued forth, Gyles caught up John's arm and wrenched it high, eliciting a yelp. "What've you done with her? Adelaide!"

A moan met his ears.

"Where?" He poked puny John in the ribs with his pistol.

"Here! Here!" The little man scampered like a child to the back stall and rushed in to stand, panting, against the rotting wooden frame.

"My darling," Heath crooned to her as he lifted her up from the hay. Never in all his life would he forget the pitiful sight of his beloved, her horrified blue eyes stark with fright and wild relief; her pretty apple green gown torn and dirtied; her body trussed up at her feet and bound by the wrists with rough old rope. Before he killed the man who'd done this to her, Gyles unwound the rough hemp wound around her mouth and neck, then sheltered her in his embrace. "Come here, sweetheart."

SHE LAY IN Gyles's arms for blessed long minutes as he muttered senseless comforts to her. She didn't care what he said, she knew only his solace and the safety of his presence. What he asked, she had no answers for. What he required, she had no idea. What she wanted was only to stand once more and to confront the putrid little pego who had the gall to put a stinking potion to her nose and make her swoon like a cut flower under his hand. She did not wilt for any man. This violent fellow would pay.

That was all she could think of.

So when at last Gyles helped her to stand on her own two feet and he ran his warm seductive hands along her ribs and hips, she began to think of how he might do that in some other place, some finer time with more delightful intentions than he had at this particular moment. With that, she knew she was recovering her senses.

At the moment, Gyles began a diatribe against the little twit who had the audacity to manhandle her person. Did God know if he'd handled her very fine person more than he should? She didn't.

But she couldn't, wouldn't, allow that lack to destroy the safety Gyles brought her. Not now. Gyles was here to think for her.

But she had her own relevant statements to make to this idiot who had abducted her.

"Thank you, my darling," she whispered to Gyles and kissed his cheek. "I am so glad you found me."

"I will always find you, my sweet. You are my own."

"I am indeed." She tried to smile at him, but her lips were cracked, and her cheeks were sore. So much for looking like the rescued damsel. For her hurt, she whirled toward the silly man who had done this foul deed.

"You, John Fellowes, are a disgrace." She pushed away from her beloved and wobbled but stood steady. Then she stepped toward the little heathen, who held himself up with the aid of the stable wall. "You profess to love people, and yet you took me in broad daylight. You should be brought before a court to stand trial for such a crime."

From the corner of the stall, an older man who looked far too like John to not be related groaned. "He is my boy."

"He is my abductor," she spat. "If I find that you have abused me or used me in a foul manner, I shall have the law on you."

"I never touched you! I wanted to marry you. Marry you!"

Gyles snarled. "You are not worthy to touch her shoes."

"Why?" The little curate stuck his neck out. "You'll take her even if she's been soiled?"

Gyles reached around her to grab the man, but she forced his arm down.

"She is to be my wife, you snail."

The cur laughed. "I could've had 'er. You did. At the Carstairs'."

"Never say it," Gyles growled. "Never even breathe it. Mark my words, if you so much as hint at what has happened here today, I will hound you to the ends of the earth. I will tell it far and wide that you defiled your calling. That you abducted a young woman. You won't be a curate. Or a rector. You'll never get a living."

"Now...now, see here," the earl stuttered and shook a finger in Gyles's face.

"Put that away, sir," Gyles ordered him. "You know not to whom you speak. But rest assured, if you so much as look as if you are about to tell a sordid tale of abduction and capture or rape, you will hang as well as your son."

The earl gulped and shrank backward.

"Come along, my darling." Heath bent to lift her into his arms.

But she put up a hand to stall him. "One thing, Heath."

"Heath?" asked the stableboy.

"Heath," confirmed the earl.

The name of her rescuer's identity caused many to exclaim and grumble.

"As you wish, my love." Gyles raised both hands and let her

walk toward the culprit who had so wronged her.

She stared at Fellowes for a long minute. "It is a pity that you have no ethics, sir. A crime you have no morals, either. Worse, I would suggest you find a new profession. It does not suit you. I will ensure it does not. Ever. In quiet little ways, you will remember me and what you did here, and at everything you try, you will fail. As you did here. As you will do everywhere you go."

She took one step from him.

But on second thought turned to face him again.

She indulged herself. She did the one thing she'd learned from a kindly old pirate shipwrecked upon the Waterford shore.

She rounded on her attacker like a bare-knuckle boxer and punched John Fellowes smack in the nose. Better, she made him bleed.

The little man screamed and clutched his bulbous proboscis as red blood gushed through his fingers.

The four men gasped.

Gyles, murmuring his approval, took her arm and led her toward the private stables next door to that of the Davenports'. There, he hailed the grooms and asked if he might borrow the owners' city coach for the afternoon. Off the two went to the house to ask if the Marquess of Heath might avail himself of the gentleman's conveyance. The man agreed, and Gyles paid a handsome sum for the privilege.

"I will not have you ride a horse," Gyles explained to her. "You need care, my dearest."

Within minutes, he led her up into the welcome appointments of plush squabs, shades drawn, for a private ride home to Charles Street. His three friends saw them off, assuring Gyles they would see his stallion returned to his new house.

Inside, he curled his arms around her and brought her safe and secure to rest upon his lap.

She nestled against him, laughter tickling her that she'd been naughty to Fellowes at the end. "I had to hit him."

"I do agree, my darling. A wonderful job you did of it, too."

"I wanted to strike him on the jaw."

"No matter. A fine jab."

"Thank you. But he has such a little chin. Nothing to land on, you see. And he has such a blunderbuss of a nose."

Gyles finally laughed, and sobering, he lifted her chin. "I've settled all my business in London."

"You came at the right time."

He threaded his fingers through her long soft tresses, then thumbed her lower lip. "I want you with me always. I love you, sweetheart, and I've come back to marry you. I obtained a license, too. Will you truly have me, Adelaide Devereaux?"

She kissed his appealing mouth. Now was no time to ask about his parents' objection to her as his wife. "I cannot wait to have you for my own."

"How does tomorrow suit you?"

She cupped his cheek and grinned. "Before noon."

"And after that, we'll be together for the rest of our lives."

※※※

GYLES TOOK HER home to her cousin Cass and her sister Laurel. His friends returned his horse and joined them minutes later. Colonel Lord Welles, whom Cass hailed with tears in her eyes, added a few details of Addy's abduction that Gyles had not yet learned. Captain Fitzroy was his jovial self, accepting a bracing glass of brandy along with the offer of dinner. Lord Grey was welcomed, even by Laurel, whom he had jilted long ago.

Soon after Cass and Laurel had exclaimed over Addy's rescue and assured themselves of Addy's fitness and John Fellowes's defeat, Gyles requested a private audience with Addy. She readily took his hand. Cass approved, her glance checking Gyles's for his good intentions.

The two of them retired to the small salon on the first floor, where he closed and locked the door, then swept his darling up into his fast embrace and strode with her to the far settee.

He took her on his lap and cupped her cheek. "You are truly recovered?"

"I am. Oh, Gyles, he was quite pitiful."

"Resourceful chap to take you in broad daylight. I will make my appreciation known to your French maid for identifying the bastard. Pardon me, my darling, for my language."

"But he is not fit for any profession, least of all *that* one."

"So true. Now," he said as he smiled into her eyes and brushed her lips with the pad of his thumb. "Are you ready to hear all my news?"

She frowned, and he kissed her quickly. My God, she had such wonderful plush lips. When he drew away, she still had her eyes closed, and he had to taste her once more.

"Ohh." She breathed and fell back in his arms. "How wonderful to have you back."

"I couldn't agree more," he crooned and pushed her to the cushions, then followed her down. "I've wanted you forever, and I must have you as my wife. But is tomorrow too soon?"

She kissed him, opening her mouth for him and allowing him to roam and savor the taste of her. "Never. I want you. Always have. Since the first night you danced with me, I saw no one else."

"Kissed no one else?" he asked in a playful tone.

"Not one." She fastened her gaze on his.

He caught her nape and held her still. That she could be his, stunned him. That he could love this madly, shocked him. "Will you have me for your husband?"

"I will! I will! No other!" She ran her fingers into his hair and clutched him close. Her breasts, tight little buds that poked his chest, rubbed against him even as her arms bound him close. But she looked fearful. "Tell me what you did in London."

"I pensioned off one mistress."

She scowled.

He drew his fingertip over the line on her forehead. "I had

not gone to her for months. It was time I did the honorable thing by her and gave her money to live. Just as I did the other one months ago."

Addy's mouth fell open.

"They are irrelevant, my darling. I want no others ever. I promise you fidelity."

She took a moment to process that. "As I promise you."

He hugged her close and smiled. "I've acquired that license to marry, which we can use as soon as you wish."

"I do wish for tomorrow."

"You shall have what you want."

"You!" she said, joy shining in her eyes.

He splayed his fingers into the long silken strands of her glorious hair. "All of me."

She frowned. "What of your father? His objection to me. I heard of it. Will he stop you?"

"I've secured the best legal advice, and he cannot object. Not on the grounds he presented to me. My father might wish to object to signing the documents to approve of your dowry and settlement. He might not want to sign to make you the legitimate spouse of the marquess to become the next duchess. Yesterday, I had my solicitor send him my own stipulations with the documents my father must sign. You see, I have, for many years, supported my father's lavish spending with funds from my own earnings. I have cut those off unless he signs."

"Your father can survive without your help?"

That she could show compassion for his father's welfare at this juncture had Gyles loving her all the more for it. "He can and will. Furthermore, he should. He spends far too much. As to the painting he seeks that is supposedly in your grandfather's collection, there is no record of him offering a family heirloom, a portrait to be exact, as collateral for a debt. If he sold a painting or gave it away, he was remiss not to record it in the family estate records. Trust me, everything of any value is always cataloged in those books. It is my father's word, only, that he sold away the

Holbein portrait of the Countess of Stonegage."

Addy shook her head. "Hans Holbein?"

"The name of the artist who supposedly painted a portrait of a Stonegage lady, yes."

"Laurel might know. She knows all sorts of things about Grandpapa."

"I care not." He'd settled that issue with his father and the solicitor, and he would not revisit the matter. Affirmed in that, he sent the bodice of her gown down over one perfect breast. Kissing every inch of her beautiful body would be his new daily ambition. "This, I do care about."

She wiggled beneath him, encouraging him to bend to her and take her in his mouth. "Ohh. I must have more of this."

He smiled against her skin. She would be a daunting bed partner, a daring lover, and a wife to savor for the rest of his life.

The dazzling vision of how they would be entangled together for the rest of their lives had him withdrawing his hand and covering all her charms. "Tomorrow, my darling. We will finish this."

Chapter Thirteen

T HE WEDDING DAY dawned bright and hot, a perfect day, Addy thought, after such a terrible start yesterday. She chose for her wedding the white gown she'd worn to the musicale a few nights ago. Happy to be wed so soon after Imogen, she dressed with Fifi's help and happily chatted away with Laurel as Fifi corseted her so tightly, she thought she'd never breathe again.

Addy turned this way and that in the cheval glass. "Loosen those stays, Fifi."

"Zis gown," the French woman groused, "it will not fit."

"It will. Not to worry. Once I am at home in the country with Gyles, I'll give up corsets forever!"

Fifi feigned a gasp. "Scandal!"

Laurel chuckled. "Good for you. You'll be far enough away from society, they'll never know you are...ahem...*free* of all restraints!"

"On a serious note, I do want you to visit me."

Laurel looked not at all disturbed that she was the last Devereaux triplet left on the shelf. She beamed at Addy, her jade eyes twinkling in happiness for her. "Never doubt that I will. You will have to usher me out the door, I will be such a bother."

Addy whirled and threw her arms around her sister. "Never a bother. You are our oldest, our wisest."

"Now, now. Don't go too far. We have yet to see how I get on." She plunked down into a slipper chair. Her pretty Chinese jade silk gown a complement to the red of her hair and ivory skin.

Addy turned back, picking up long diamond ear bobs that Gyles had brought from London from his heirloom vaults and given her yesterday. She had to let Laurel know her chances for a good marriage still existed. Perhaps more so in the past few days. "Lord Grey was pleasant to you yesterday."

Laurel stilled, the flash of longing for her first love irrepressible. "He's here for the rest of the Season, he tells me."

"And without his family." Grey's father had been the one to demand that he withdraw his suit and leave Laurel with the scandal of being jilted.

"He came to Dublin without them years ago. That is no sign that he's free from their influence."

Addy caught a view of Laurel in the reflection in her mirror. "Yesterday, he was helpful to Gyles."

"Good of him. They are friends." Laurel rolled a shoulder. "Of course, Hadley would help rescue his friend's fiancée."

"You still think of him so dearly that you call him Hadley." *Grey's first name fits him,* Addy thought. Easy to say. Easy to be with. Still, he had cruelly left her sister to pine for him and hate him and regret him.

They fell into a silence as Addy finished dressing.

When she twirled once more before the long glass, Laurel stood and came behind her to give her a hug and kiss her on the cheek. "Always remember Imogen and I were your first friends, your closest confidants, and—"

"My finest trouble makers!"

They laughed, and when they parted, each wiped a tear from their lashes.

"I will write to Imogen tonight with all the details. Come now, let's see you married to this very handsome man."

"My marquess who does not care that I come from that Irish family with the shady name."

"Or that your sisters are…" Laurel waved a hand without words to describe their slightly indiscreet notoriety.

"Talented in very odd ways?" Addy looped her arm through Laurel's as they headed toward the hall and stairs. "A little light-fingered?"

Laurel waggled hers. "Yes. We play piano well."

Addy nodded. "Or sing on key?"

"Only when we wish to impress a beau."

Addy snickered. "Or when we need to imitate someone's signature?"

Laurel stopped in her tracks, boring a hole in Addy's gaze. "We're not good at that at all."

Addy searched her sister's expression. Whatever did she mean? Was there a technicality Addy had missed? Or was she just wrong about Laurel's unique skill? Addy patted her hand. "All right then. Forget that."

"We're going to a wedding," Laurel said. "And the only thing that matters is that we are all happy."

"Very happy." Addy squeezed her sister's arm and marched down the stairs to her new tomorrow.

><><

THE RECTOR WAS nervous. The groom was jubilant. The bride was deliriously happy.

Addy looked about at those who stood toasting Gyles and her, and she rejoiced in the excitement of her wedding day. Cousin Cass had not only managed to invite twenty-five friends, but she had, with Gyles's approval, sent over a special invitation to the Duke and Duchess of Stonegage. Both attended and appeared not only regal but resigned to accepting their new daughter-in-law.

Addy was gracious and correct in polite conversation with them. Gyles was watchful and protective, his hand at her waist, his words to his parents polite if not quite cordial. He had left her yesterday and told her he would see his father and mother that evening and take Cass's invitation. If they chose to come was their decision.

Colonel Lord Welles was in attendance and spent the morning reception mostly at Cass's side. Lord Grey spoke a few times with Laurel, but their conversation appeared to Addy to be brief and congenial. But when Captain Fitzroy took up the conversation with Laurel for most of the breakfast, Grey appeared envious.

Addy took all that as a very good sign.

"Time for us to go, my darling," Gyles reminded her for the second time.

Off they went in a flurry of everyone applauding and laughing.

"HERE WE ARE, Marchioness. Home for a few weeks." He climbed down from his coach and offered Addy his hand. Expecting he would need days or weeks to propose properly to Addy and set their wedding date, he had asked her if she wished to go elsewhere for their honeymoon. But she'd said anywhere with him alone would be perfect.

"Exactly my thought," he'd replied.

Now she took one look at the grand stucco house and gave a smile of approval. "It's lovely."

The butler, a man who was employed by the earl who owned the house, was an efficient no-nonsense type. He had arranged for a cold buffet supper in the upstairs parlor and hot baths for both Addy and Gyles. Meanwhile, Reginald James, who was Gyles's valet, had put the finishing touches to both master and mistress's bedrooms sorting and hanging clothes. A maid for Addy had been hired from the local registry office. She appeared to be a shy young thing with few opinions, very opposite Fifi.

Gyles awaited his bride in the small salon upstairs where the butler and staff had laid out a rather extensive selection of cheeses and meats, cold lettuces and radishes, and a few small cakes. The sun set before Addy appeared.

She came through the adjoining door to her suite and eyed him in his emerald green banyan. "My, you look so handsome," she told him and came to place her hands over his heart.

He pressed her hands to his chest and let his gaze absorb her. "You, my love, are even more beautiful than I have ever imagined."

And she was. In the white silk robe that flowed over her lithe figure, with her hair drifting to her waist, her blue eyes shining, she was ethereal.

"May I serve you, or do you prefer to select yourself?" he asked.

"I will do it." She curved a finger under his jaw. "First, I wish to sit and talk with you."

At that invitation, he laughed and took her up in his arms. For to make love to her would be so easy. Easy as loving her had always been. He strode with her to the chaise lounge and settled her in his lap.

But to his surprise, she had tears in her eyes. He put his lips to her lashes. "My darling, what is wrong?"

"I fear I've caused you a lot of trouble. Yesterday with that horrid little man. And well, you see, I don't wish to cause you more."

He brushed away another tear and brought her warm, soft body close to his heart. "You will not, ever."

"But I am not like other women."

He inhaled the lavender scent from her bath, and his body surged to life in want. "I know you're not. You are unique, my sweet wife." He longed to lay her down on the broad bed he'd admired in the master suite and show her just how unique she was. Biding his time and pleasing her, he smiled and massaged her shoulders. That only brought her breasts closer to him, and her hard dark nipples jutted out from the silk. He was damn tempted but schooled himself to be respectful and not touch her until she was ready for him.

She cupped his cheek and was in earnest. "Oh, my dear husband, I must tell you who I am. What I am."

He worried that she would make some silly confession, irrelevant to his love for her. "Addy, I know who you are."

"No, no. Listen to me, Gyles. It is very burdensome to be beautiful."

He swallowed the bark of laughter that rose in his throat. Hearing such a statement from any other woman, he would have let himself go. But Addy was stunning, and she did try to manage her condition. That she was so blunt about it enchanted him even more than he already was. So, he tried to be diplomatic. "I'm sure it is, my darling."

"Most men think you are…a…a fruit!"

Apt that. His Addy was a juicy strawberry, a crisp apple or… "A peach?"

"Exactly." She sniffed.

He wiped an errant tear from her lashes as she wiggled in his lap and set his cock to hardening. "Ripe."

"Very. And then they think you have no thought, no ambition, or talent except catering to them."

He pushed a silken curl from her cheek. "Idiocy."

"Precisely. What sort of woman settles for a man who takes her for a…a mindless…?"

"Peach?"

She nodded. "Imogen always said men saw only her breasts."

Dear God. "They do?"

Addy pressed her lips together and nodded quickly. "They are large, you know."

He had noticed her sister's ripe figure but had not found it what he most remembered about that funny lady. Being at heart a diplomat—and one should with a woman commenting on another's form—he searched for his glass near at hand and picked it up to take a sip of wine.

Addy went on. "She said it was disconcerting to find that they constantly looked not at her eyes but at the points of her nipples."

Gyles choked on his drink. "Terrible."

"Men were always going on about my skin or my hair. Men don't love women...truly love any woman...for her hair."

"Never."

She sat up a little and looked him straight in the eyes. "You don't love my hair, do you?"

"It suits you." Bright. Full of sunlight, the essence of her cheerful character. "But no, I'm not in love with your hair. You could go bald, and I'd never notice."

She shivered. "That's a truly frightening picture."

He shook his head and pointed to hers. "I love what's *in* your head, my darling."

"Oh, good." She settled back into his arms.

"More than that," he whispered as he placed his palm between her breasts, "I love what's in here."

"Show me."

>>>><<<<

ADDY WANTED HIM to make love to her. She wished to be taken, possessed as her husband's true and loving equal. Certainly, she'd seen no hint in his eyes or words from his lips that he feared Fellowes had ruined her. But she worried.

Oh, yes, last night she had examined her clothes that she'd worn yesterday when that horrid little man abducted her. The bodice of her walking dress was intact. The skirts of her gown and petticoats were not torn. The hems of both were soiled, showing no greater signs of use than her walk to the Lanes. Indeed, the garments bore few marks for the way he had manhandled her. They were wrinkled. A few bits of hay had worked their way into the warp and weft of her cotton dress and muslin petticoats. But her drawers were intact. No blood marked the fine fabric.

She was not sore. She was not marked on her breasts or her intimate places. Her fear that he had raped her in the stables abated but still lived as a possibility. She wished to be whole for her husband.

"Marchioness!" He grinned at her, driving her sorrows farther away. "Where do you go without me?"

She must not stay here to say this. She pushed up and away to walk toward the fireplace. She had to face him—and spun. "I am afraid we might discover I am not whole."

Alarm did not crease his brows. He was cool, centered, focused on her expression.

"Do you have evidence of this?"

"None."

"Why then are you apprehensive?"

"I do want to be perfect for you."

"We all want to be perfect, my love. But that is a fine ambition and a life-long process."

She frowned, catching up the silk of her nightclothes and rubbing the gossamer in her nervous fingers. He was being obtuse when, surely, he knew what she meant by her need for perfection. "I did nothing to encourage him."

"I know that."

"In fact, I was rude."

He gave her a crooked little smile. "So I assumed."

"He was insulting to you, too. And saw us..." She could not look at Gyles any longer.

"Come to me."

She considered the Aubusson rug and shook her head.

"Do. Come." He waggled his fingers at her.

She went to stand before him but could not meet his gaze.

"I love you."

She caught the sob that rose in her throat.

"You love me, too."

She let out the cry that erupted from her. "Very much!"

He took up her hand and put her fingertips to his lips. His

breath was warm, his word warmer. "I doubt he had the courage to take you."

"I agree."

He took one of her fingertips between his teeth and held. "I doubt he had the strength to force you."

"He had the strength to pick me up and take me away in his father's carriage."

Gyles hummed his agreement. But then he took another finger of hers and laved it with his tongue. His little caress soothed her down to her core. "From what Grey told me of his altercation with the man before he left the house, the little fellow had his coachman and a footman help him."

"The cur!" She fisted both hands, but the one Gyles held was graced with a nip to yet a third fingertip.

"If you see no ruin to the clothes you wore yesterday, and you feel no discomfort in your body, then, my darling, you are well."

She met his mellow brown gaze with the hope he was correct. "I will die if I'm not."

"Oh, Addy." He reached up and dropped a trail of kisses from her fingers to her wrist up to her elbow.

She swayed toward him.

Catching her, he wrapped his arms around her to bring her close. "Please don't die, my sweet. I want you with me for years and years."

She splayed her fingers into the wealth of his soft auburn hair. "I'd like that."

"Then allow me, my darling, to prove to you that you are my honored wife."

She cupped his nape and bent to kiss him.

He took her to him and set her over his legs, hers to each side of his. Then with the arch of a wicked red brow, he locked his eyes on hers and raised the negligee over her legs. With his hands spread wide upon her thighs, he met her gaze frankly. "You have no memory of his hands on you."

She shook her head.

He caressed her inner thighs. "And no memory of his reassembling his clothes."

"No."

He raised her skirts higher and the night air cooled her exposed intimate flesh. "You recall no attempt by him to touch you." He trailed a finger down her seam.

She grabbed her breath. "No."

"Not here?" He opened her wide with the fingers of one hand. And with fingers of the other, found the nubbin he had loved with his tongue nights before.

Her eyes fell closed. "No. Not there. Only you."

He sank two hot fingers inside her core.

"Only you," she breathed, arching back to take more of him.

"Only me." He curved his fingers around inside her.

She gulped in frantic need. Somewhere, somehow, he'd lost the satin banyan. She saw him naked before her. A dashing sight. His passion molten and urgent on his face. His body supple. And within reach, his manhood huge and rigid.

"I'm yours," he told her in that dark voice of possession. "Take me in hand, and I will show you."

Her hand shook, but her mind was firm. Eager. Hungry. She circled her hand around his rod.

He covered her hand and urged her to massage him.

She watched him, her husband of hours, as he taught her the way to pleasure him. And in the pleasuring, she gushed with her own desire for him and could do naught but pant.

"Come closer," he whispered. "Now, put me inside you."

She wiggled closer, needy, delirious to have him.

Her head fell back at the heat of him, the size, the rapture of him.

He inched forward and back.

"No! Don't go"

He gave a little laugh and drove inside her further.

"Oh. That. Is. Ahhhh."

He chuckled. Then he stood with her in his arms, and with his manhood firmly inside her, he strolled. Oh my, did he saunter to the bed, and there he sat with her atop him and pushed himself more deeply inside her.

"You are talented, my husband."

"You give me inspiration, my wife."

She licked her lips. "Can I give you more?"

He hooted. "Eternally!" At once, he rolled her to the linens and pushed her up to spread her on the bed. In the doing, he had left her.

She glanced down to see how he still stood high and proud and wanting. But she also saw the evidence that she had been whole, untouched, her innocence given only to her husband. She smiled up at him, and he grinned, rejoicing with her. "Will you come inside again, please?"

He took himself in hand and slowly sank inside her, and at his hilt, she wept two happy tears.

She was not sore. She was not pained.

"I love you," she whispered.

He showed her by his tenderness that he claimed her as his mate.

"My love, my everything," he said against her ear after she had been spent, and he had, too.

>>>«««

THROUGH THE NIGHT, he took her to new vistas, each with utmost care. Sitting in the bed, her elegant legs spread wide in abandon, he took her slowly to a new paradise he discovered with her. Hours later, the dawn sunlight shimmering over her gilded torso, he showed her the way to quick hard rapture. At midday, he arranged her just so and performed the act that had so excited him and her the night of the musicale.

No woman had ever satisfied him like this.

She grasped him to her afterward and did him the compliment to come a second time with him inside her. She was his darling, generous and giving. He drew away, exhausted, proud of his foresight to leave his vain pursuits behind and marry her.

At noon, he rose and rang the pull for his valet.

He ordered coffee and a full breakfast. One large bath. For two, he thought.

Afterward, his wife slept for an hour or more, her arms flat upon the linens, snoring. He watched her, laughing at the symphony of her snorts, and when she woke herself up, he went to her. "Have I tired you completely, my darling?"

"I need sustenance. Coffee. Strawberry pie, preferably, but whatever Cook has to hand."

"You shall have it."

"You, too, sir." She pushed up on an elbow, the sheet falling to reveal how keen she remained for his attentions. "I hope we are not finished with my lessons."

"Never!" He hovered over her.

"Good." She shook back her hair, held him there with a hand to his nape, and let him enjoy himself. "I asked Imogen to tell me if she and Lex had...you know...done this."

He raised his head. The taste of her skin was better than any wine. "You did?"

"I did. They hadn't. So...you see...you have to show me all the ways to make you happy."

"To make us both happy? Oh, I will do that." He went back to putting his tongue to her breast.

"Mmm. That's lovely. What of the other one? You'll kiss me there?"

"Darling?" He locked his gaze on hers.

"Yes?"

"Do be quiet and let me focus on my instructions."

She squirmed. "Go to it."

"Thank you."

And he did.

Chapter Fourteen

A FEW AUTUMN leaves of red and gold fell upon the window ledge outside their bedroom suite before they ventured out to be seen by others. They were on their honeymoon and enjoyed the seclusion. Two weeks after their wedding, Addy invited Laurel and Cass to dinner. The next week, she invited her sister and cousin again, plus Lord Grey and Captain Fitzroy, to even the numbers. Colonel Lord Welles was unavailable, having ridden off to Berkshire last week when a letter arrived for him at his lodgings that his father, the Duke of Ruscombe, was ailing badly.

Cass did not speak of Welles in private. Laurel said naught about her current relationship with Grey, if, indeed, they were now more than acquaintances. Addy noted the four guests conversed easily at the table, and so she was content not to ask her relatives for any details.

She had asked Gyles if he wished to have his parents to dine, but he had dismissed the idea. "One day, perhaps. Papa still has ambitions of obtaining that Holbein, and I will not have him resurrect the matter. Not to me and certainly not to you."

From Grandpapa's estate manager, Addy had no new information on the disposal of the old gentleman's private collection. Gyles declared he wished her not to question the estate manager. "My father's desire to have the painting was nothing more than a convenience to object to my marrying you. He signed the papers to acknowledge you, and that is as it should be. I'll countenance no more of his focus on family scandals and inter-family rivalries. You are mine, and I am yours, and he will accept it absolutely."

That, too, she applauded, and worried no more one day the Duke of Stonegage would come for her and some artwork he wished to seize simply by mere declaration.

"Shall we go to London soon?" he asked her one morning as she emerged from her boudoir and her bath. Frowning, he quickly folded the newspaper he read.

"I think so. We should call upon a few people as a married couple. I also want to find a few apothecaries whom Mister Algood recommends. For samples for my remedies, of course, to take home to Yorkshire with us when we go north. I'd like to make excellent ones to help the tenants in their maladies." She examined the gowns in her wardrobe and picked a seafoam gingham from the rack. But then, concerned about his silence, she put it back and turned to examine him. "What's the news of the day that fails to please you?"

He rose from his chair and went to stand by the fireplace. The day was hot, and they needed no fire in the house.

Addy went to him, her dressing gown billowing around her in her stride. "What's wrong?"

"Nothing wrong, really. In fact, quite right."

She took his arm and circled round him. "Tell me."

"In the 'News of the Ton' column in the *Chronicle* there is an article about those who are departing Southhampton for Baltimore in America."

"And? Who goes?"

"John Fellowes."

"Ah." She took a depth breath and walked back toward her wardrobe. But she stood there, arms lax at her sides, with no mind for selecting finery for the day. "What is your thought on that?"

"He leaves his position as curate. Leaves the Church, I do believe."

"As he should." She had no pity for him. No scorn left in her for him, either. "He must seek his own redemption."

Her interest in what to wear lost, she whirled toward the window overlooking the small Italian garden. On a whim, she grasped the crank on the window and wound it open. A glorious fresh breeze kissed her skin, and she sighed as the heat burned away her dismay.

Her husband's arms wound round her, and he nuzzled the spot behind her ear that tickled her senses. "A good day to do something naughty, I'd say."

She turned in his embrace and ran her arms around his shoulders. "Send the servants away for the day and make love in our garden?"

The flash of interest in his brown eyes had her chuckling. "My dear, you are ingenious."

"Am I? Good. What could be more naughty than that?"

"Ha! Well, I have a few ideas." He quirked his brows, then ran his fingertips under the muslin of her dressing gown and found her aching breast.

She bit her lips to hold back a moan. "Tell them to me."

"What? You need ideas?"

She inched closer to him and hooked one naked leg around his own. He was fully dressed, but she knew he soon would not be. "I do. What have you got, sir?"

"We could take a hamper to the knolls and spread out a blanket to make love."

She choked on laughter. "In view of half of Brighton?"

He rolled his eyes. "Why not?"

"Not, indeed! What else?"

"We could stay here, and I could climb into that tub with you and find a new way to...ahem...join together."

"Ah. No. We tried that once, sir. You do not fit."

He arched his brows.

"You do not fit the tub! Me, yes. Tub, no!"

"Well, then since it is so very warm outside and the cooler

weather will be upon us, I have a superb idea."

She teased him with a skeptical grin. "What?"

"I'll take the curricle. We'll go alone. Drive west past Hove."

"And?"

"We'll rent a bathing machine from the local purveyor."

"Ohhhh! And swim!" She laughed.

"You like that idea?"

"I do! With one change."

"What?"

"I'm not taking any clothes."

He lifted her off her toes and kissed her as if he hadn't in years. "My darling wife. You are a very naughty lady."

"Only with you, my love."

"Only with me!"

About the Author

Cerise DeLand loves to write about dashing heroes and the sassy women they adore. Whether she's penning historical romances or contemporaries, she has received praise for her poetic elegance and accuracy of detail.

An award-winning author of more than 50 novels, she's been published since 1991 by Pocket Books, St. Martin's Press, Kensington and independent presses. Her books have been monthly selections of the Doubleday Book Club and the Mystery Guild. Plus she's won nominations and awards for Best Historical of the Year, Best Regency and scores of rave reviews from *Romantic Times, Affair de Coeur, Publisher's Weekly* and more.

To research, she's dived into the oldest texts and dustiest library shelves. She's also traveled abroad, trusty notebook and pen in hand, to visit the chateaux and country homes she loves to people with her own imaginary characters.

And at home every day? She loves to cook, hates to dust, goes swimming at least once a week and tries (desperately) to grow vegetables in her arid backyard in south Texas!